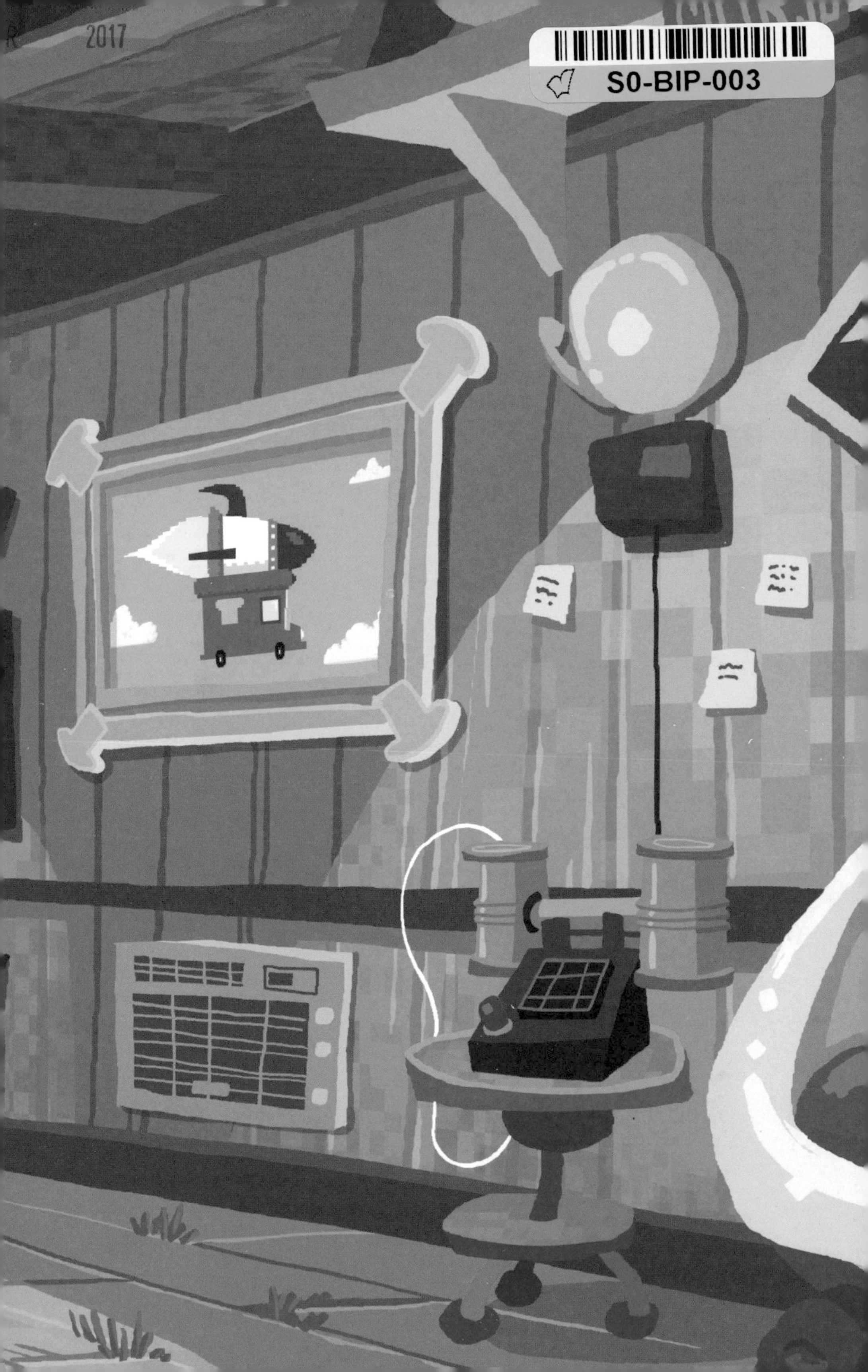

nickelodeon

BREADWINNERS™

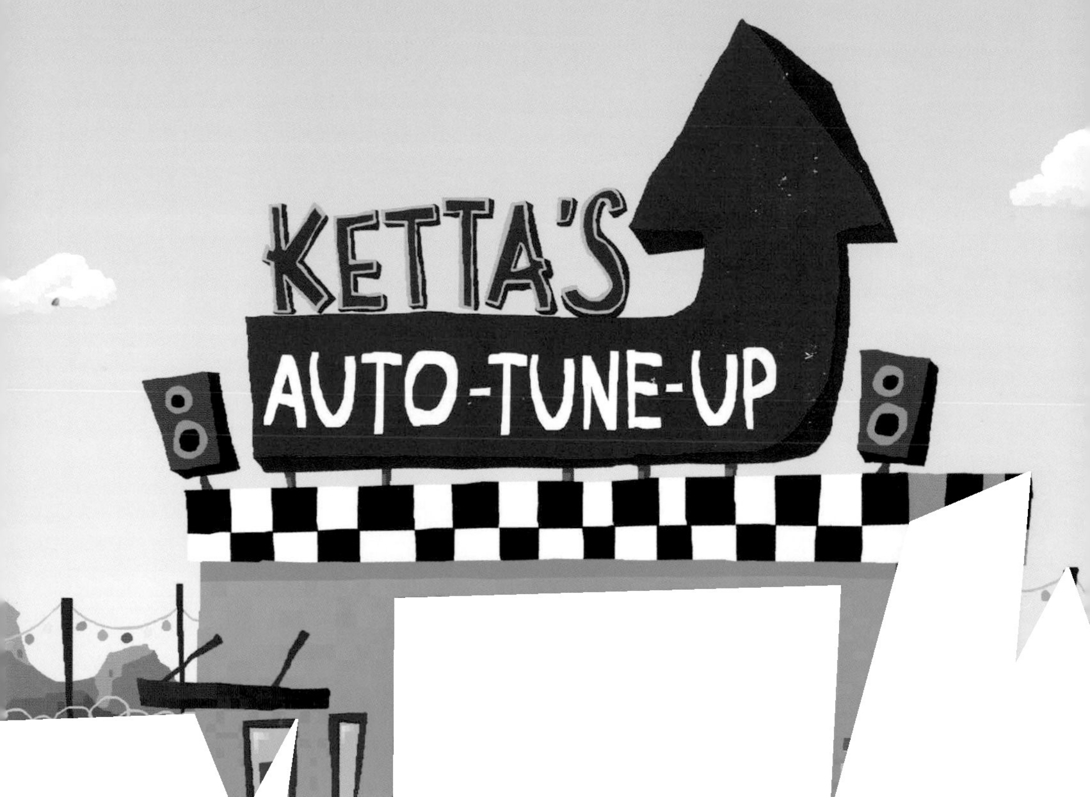
KETTA'S
AUTO-TUNE-UP

nickelodeon GRAPHIC NOVELS AVAILABLE FROM PAPERCUTZ

COMING SOO

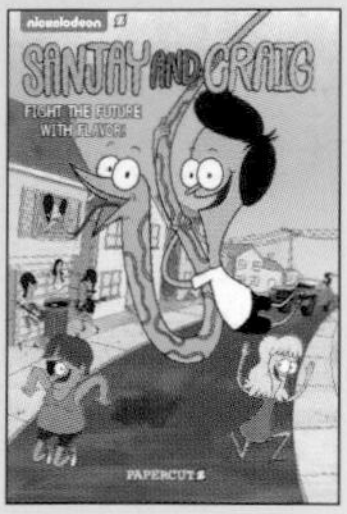
SANJAY AND CRAIG
FIGHT THE FUTURE WITH FLAVOR

#1 "Fight the Future with Flavor"

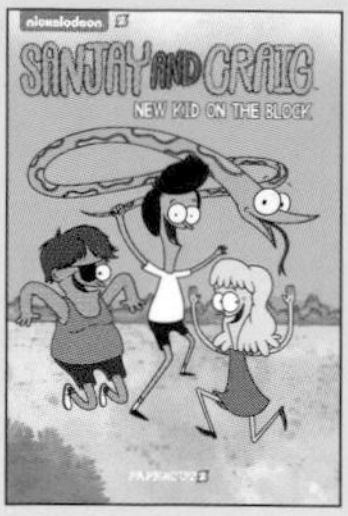
SANJAY AND CRAIG
NEW KID ON THE BLOCK

#2 "New Kid on the Block"

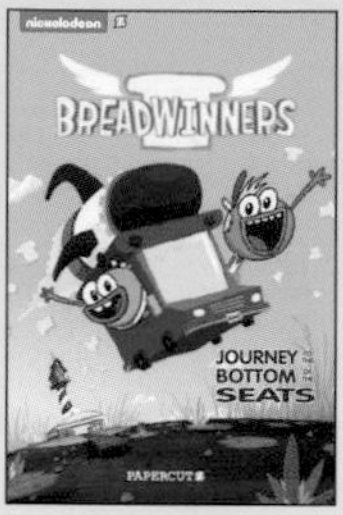
BREADWINNERS
JOURNEY TO THE BOTTOM OF THE SEATS

#1 "Journey to the Bottom of the Seats"

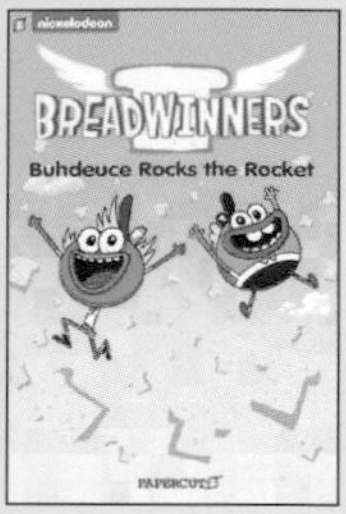
BREADWINNERS
Buhdeuce Rocks the Rocket

#2 "Buhdeuce Rocks the Rocket"

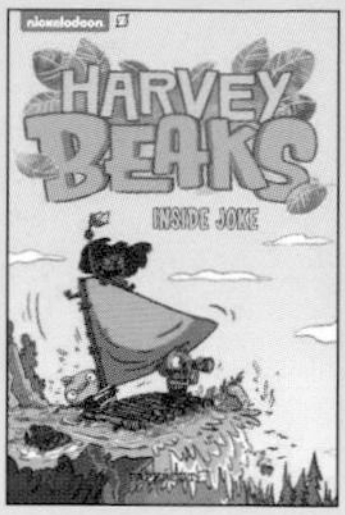
HARVEY BEAKS
INSIDE JOKE

#1 "Inside Joke"

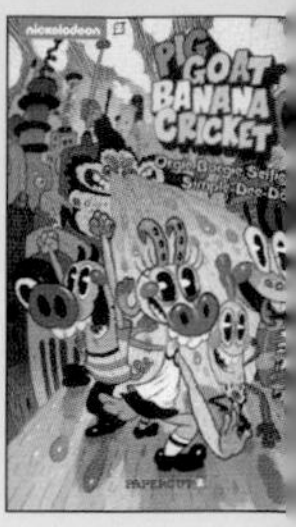
PIG GOAT BANANA CRICKET

#1 "Orgle Borgle Se Simple-Dee-Doo!"

Nickelodeon graphic novels are available for $7.99 in paperback, $12.99 in hardcover. Available from booksellers everywhere. You can also order online from Papercutz.com, or call 1-800-886-1223, Monday through Friday, 9-5 EST. MC, Visa, and AmEx accepted. To order by mail, please add $4.00 for postage and handling for first book ordered, $1.00 for each additional book and make check payable to NBM Publishing.
Send to: Papercutz, 160 Broadway, Suite 700, East Wing, New York, NY 10038.

Nickelodeon graphic novels are also available digitally wherever e-books are sold.

SUBSCRIBE!

The Greatest Kids Magazine in the world is here and you can be a charter subscriber. Be the first to get your copies and make sure you don't miss a single issue of the all-new Nickelodeon Magazine!

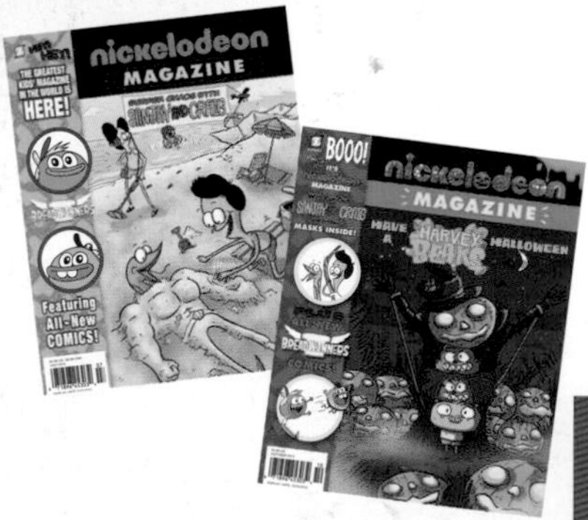
nickelodeon MAGAZINE
HERE!
Featuring All-New COMICS!
BOOO!
nickelodeon MAGAZINE
HARVEY BEAKS
HALLOWEEN

Never miss an issue of

nickelodeon MAGAZINE

Get Your Copies Delivered Right to Your Mailbox at Home

Save! And Get Free Issues

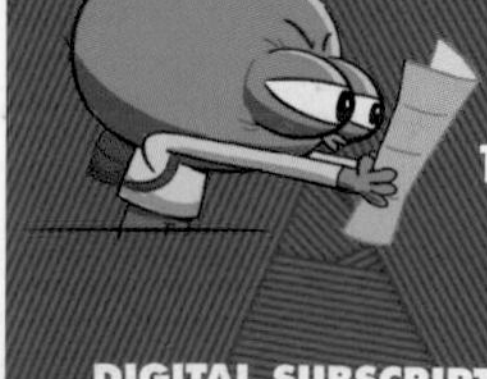

7 ISSUES FOR THE PRICE OF 6!

+SAVE $7 OFF COVER PRICE!

6 REGULAR ISSUES
+1 BONUS FREE ISSUE
7 ISSUES FOR ONLY $27.5

14 ISSUES FOR THE PRICE OF 12!

+SAVE $14 OFF COVER PRICE!

12 REGULAR ISSUES
+2 BONUS FREE ISSUES
14 ISSUES FOR ONLY $49.99

DIGITAL SUBSCRIPTION - ONLY $19.99 - OR FREE FOR ALL PRINT SUBSCRIBERS

ORDER ONLINE at Papercutz.com/nickmag

OR CALL 1-800-778-6278

(Please have debit/credit card ready)

Use promo code: BWGN2.

TABLE OF CONTENTS

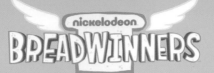

nickelodeon BREADWINNERS

#2 Buhdeuce Rocks the Rocket

"BUHDEUCE ROCKS THE ROCKET"
Stefan Petrucha – Writer
Allison Strejlau – Artist
Tom Orzechowski – Letterer
Laurie E. Smith – Colorist

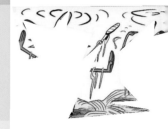

"SPAGHETTI GETAWAY"
Stefan Petrucha – Writer
Based on an idea by The Breadwinners Show Writers
Allison Strejlau – Artist
Tom Orzechowski – Letterer
Matt Herms – Colorist

"GINGERBREAD SAM"
Stefan Petrucha – Writer
Mike Kazaleh – Artist
Tom Orzechowski – Letterer
Matteo Baldrighi – Colorist

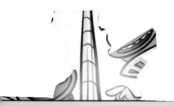

"JELLYMILK ... AMOK!"
Stefan Petrucha – Writer
Allison Strejlau – Artist
Janice Chiang – Letterer
Matt Herms – Colorist

Based on the Nickelodeon animated TV series
created by Gary "Doodles" DiRaffaele and Steve Borst

James Salerno – Sr. Art Director/Nickelodeon
Chris Nelson – Design/Production
Jeff Whitman – Production Coordinator
Bethany Bryan – Editor
Joan Hilty – Comics Editor/Nickelodeon
Asante Simons – Editorial Intern
Jim Salicrup
Editor-in-Chief

ISBN: 978-1-62991-437-4 paperback edition
ISBN: 978-1-62991-438-1 hardcover edition

Papercutz books may be purchased for business or promotional use. For information on bulk purchases please contact Macmillan Corporate and Premium Sales Department at (800) 221-7945 x5442.

Printed in China
March 2016 by O.G. Printing Productions, LTD.
26/Fl, 625 King's Road
North Point, Hong Kong
China

Distributed by Macmillan
First Printing

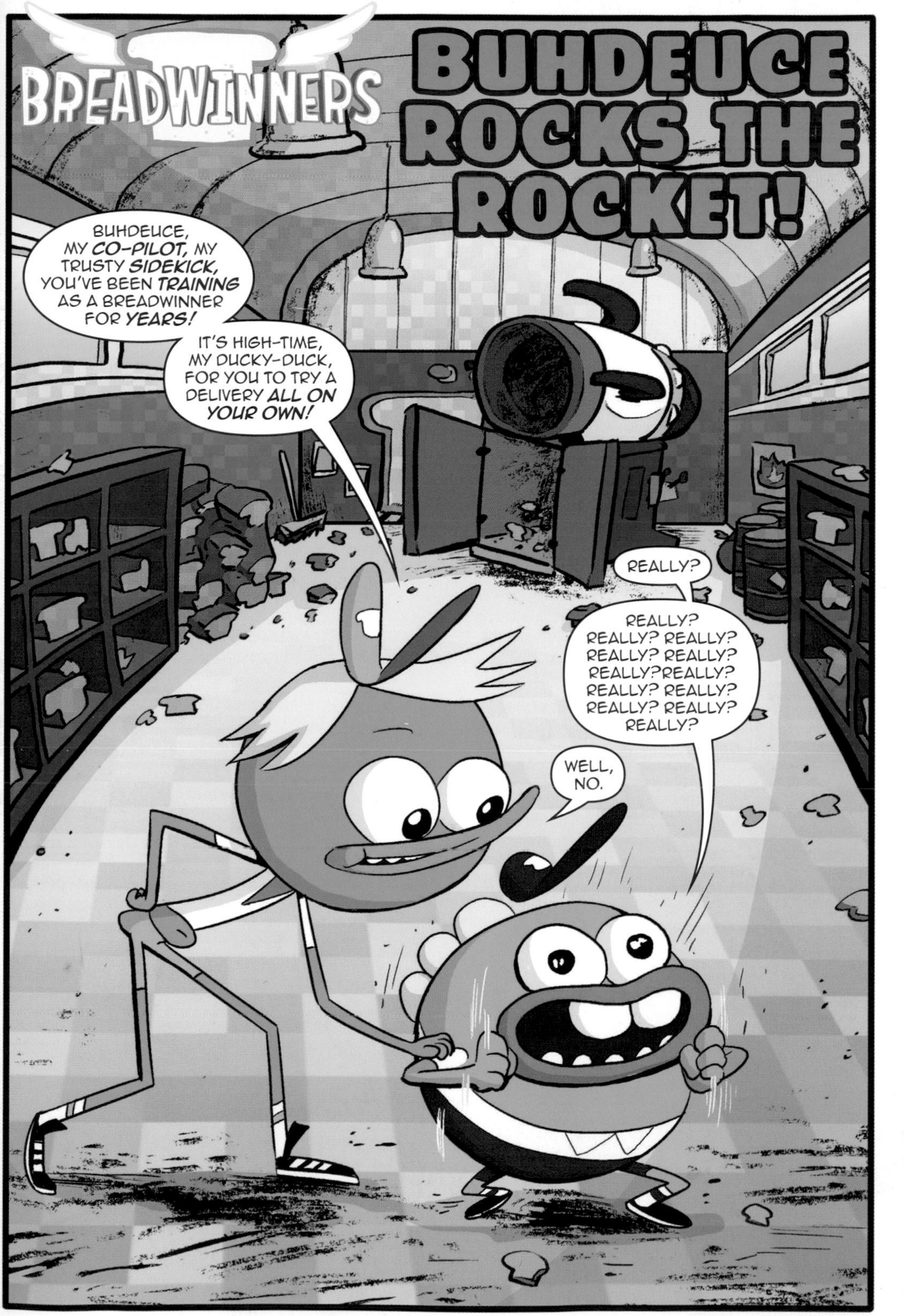
BREADWINNERS
BUHDEUCE ROCKS THE ROCKET!
BUHDEUCE, MY *CO-PILOT,* MY TRUSTY *SIDEKICK,* YOU'VE BEEN *TRAINING* AS A BREADWINNER FOR *YEARS!*
IT'S HIGH-TIME, MY DUCKY-DUCK, FOR YOU TO TRY A DELIVERY *ALL ON YOUR OWN!*
REALLY?
REALLY? REALLY? REALLY? REALLY? REALLY? REALLY?REALLY? REALLY? REALLY? REALLY? REALLY? REALLY?
WELL, NO.

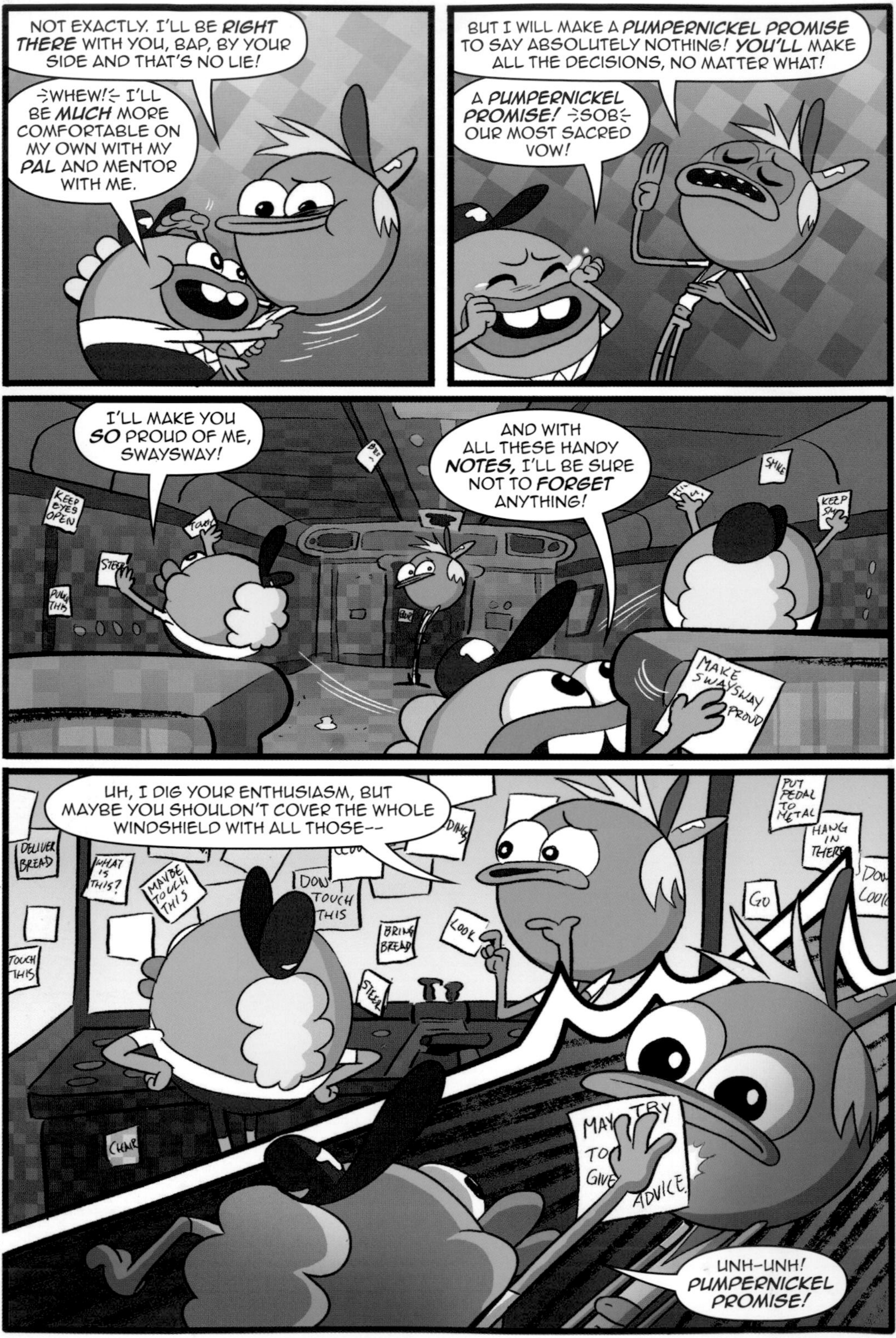
NOT EXACTLY. I'LL BE RIGHT THERE WITH YOU, BAP, BY YOUR SIDE AND THAT'S NO LIE!
WHEW! I'LL BE MUCH MORE COMFORTABLE ON MY OWN WITH MY PAL AND MENTOR WITH ME.
BUT I WILL MAKE A PUMPERNICKEL PROMISE TO SAY ABSOLUTELY NOTHING! YOU'LL MAKE ALL THE DECISIONS, NO MATTER WHAT!
A PUMPERNICKEL PROMISE! SOB OUR MOST SACRED VOW!
I'LL MAKE YOU SO PROUD OF ME, SWAYSWAY!
AND WITH ALL THESE HANDY NOTES, I'LL BE SURE NOT TO FORGET ANYTHING!
KEEP EYES OPEN
STEER
MAKE SWAYSWAY PROUD
UH, I DIG YOUR ENTHUSIASM, BUT MAYBE YOU SHOULDN'T COVER THE WHOLE WINDSHIELD WITH ALL THOSE--
PUT PEDAL TO METAL
HANG IN THERE
DELIVER BREAD
WHAT IS THIS?
MAYBE TOUCH THIS
DON'T TOUCH THIS
BRING BREAD
LOOK
GO
TOUCH THIS
STEER
MAY TRY TO GIVE ADVICE
UNH-UNH! PUMPERNICKEL PROMISE!

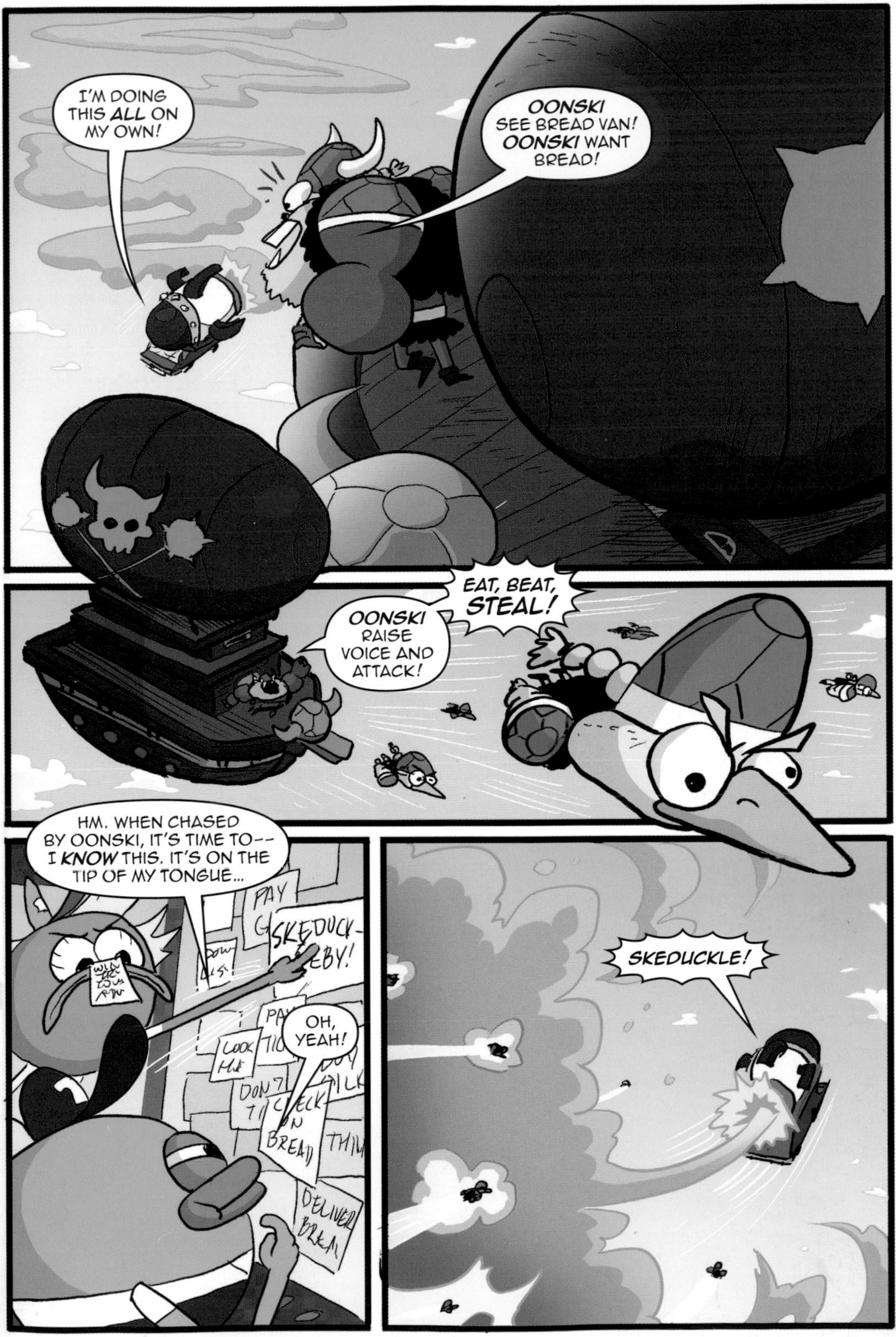
I'M DOING THIS *ALL* ON MY OWN!
OONSKI SEE BREAD VAN! *OONSKI* WANT BREAD!
OONSKI RAISE VOICE AND ATTACK!
EAT, BEAT, **STEAL!**
HM. WHEN CHASED BY OONSKI, IT'S TIME TO-- I ***KNOW*** THIS. IT'S ON THE TIP OF MY TONGUE...
CHECK ON BREAD
OH, YEAH!
SKEDUCKLE!

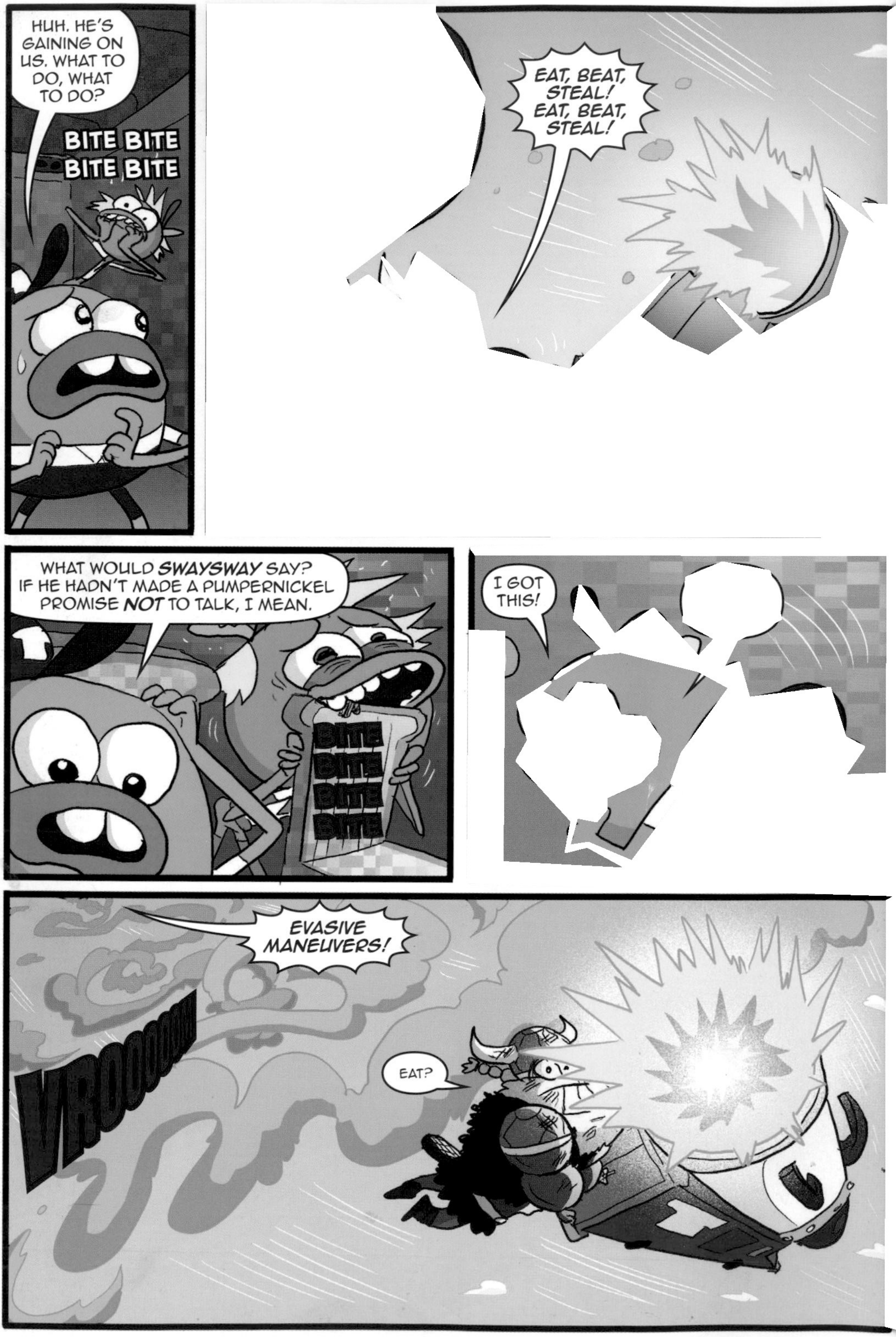
HUH. HE'S GAINING ON US. WHAT TO DO, WHAT TO DO?
BITE BITE BITE BITE
EAT, BEAT, STEAL! EAT, BEAT, STEAL!
WHAT WOULD SWAYSWAY SAY? IF HE HADN'T MADE A PUMPERNICKEL PROMISE NOT TO TALK, I MEAN.
BITE BITE BITE BITE
I GOT THIS!
EVASIVE MANEUVERS!
VROOOOOM
EAT?

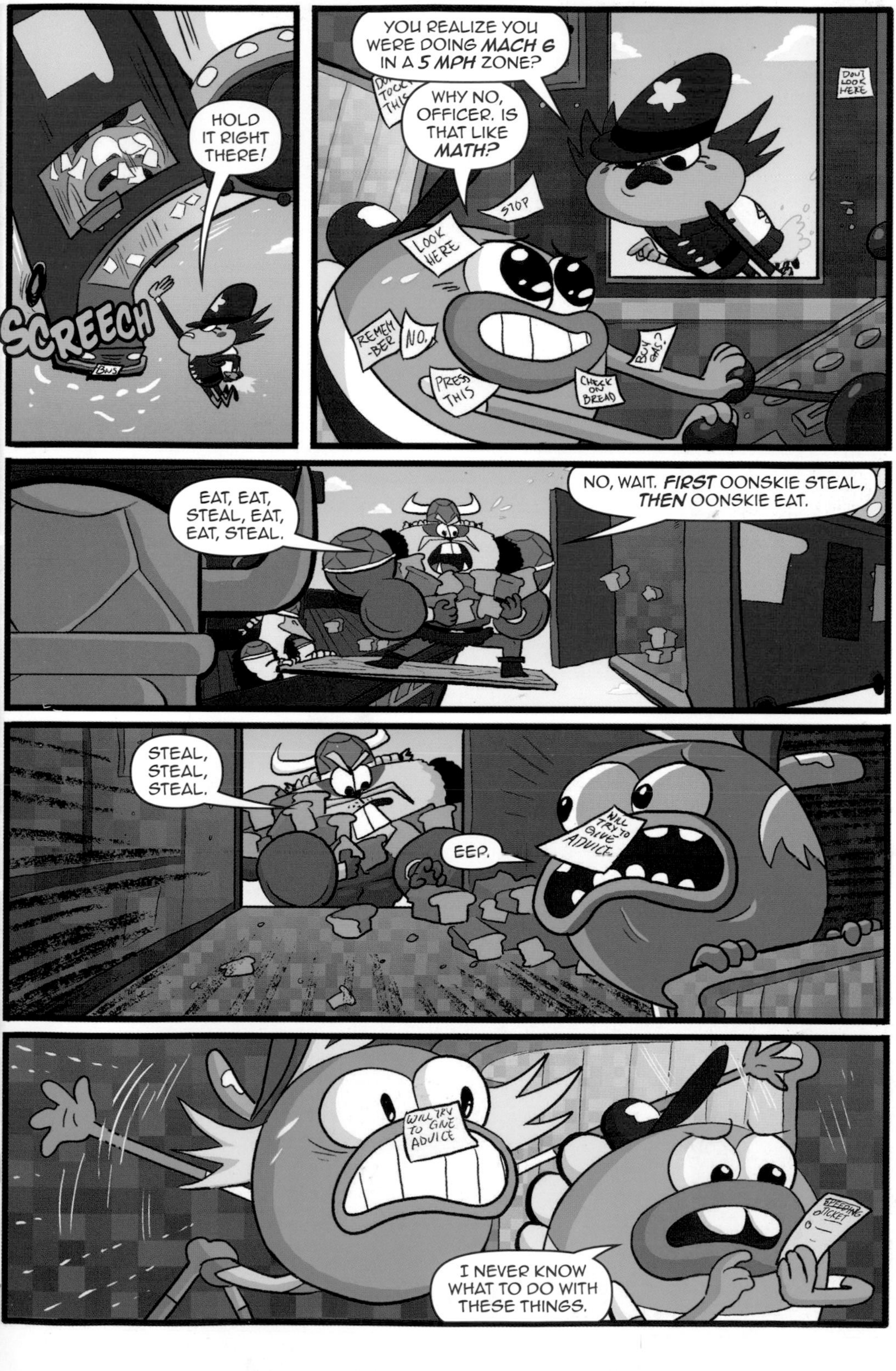
HOLD IT RIGHT THERE!
SCREECH
BUS
YOU REALIZE YOU WERE DOING MACH 6 IN A 5 MPH ZONE?
WHY NO, OFFICER. IS THAT LIKE MATH?
DON'T LOOK HERE
STOP
LOOK HERE
REMEM-BER
NO.
PRESS THIS
CHECK ON BREAD
BUY GAS?
EAT, EAT, STEAL, EAT, EAT, STEAL.
NO, WAIT. FIRST OONSKIE STEAL, THEN OONSKIE EAT.
STEAL, STEAL, STEAL.
EEP.
WILL TRY TO GIVE ADVICE
WILL TRY TO GIVE ADVICE
SPEEDING TICKET
I NEVER KNOW WHAT TO DO WITH THESE THINGS.

WHAT'S THAT, SWAYSWAY? YOU WANT TO PLAY CHARADES? OKAY.
TWO WORDS?
FIRST WORD, ONE SYLLABLE, SOUNDS LIKE HEAD? BREAD?
SECOND WORD, TWO SYLLABLES. SOUNDS LIKE... PUFFED? SWOLLEN?
HEAD SWOLLEN?
I DON'T GET IT. WHAT'S THAT SUP-POSED TO MEAN?
I'D BE HAPPY TO PLAY AGAIN ONCE I FINISH MY VERY FIRST SOLO DELIVERY.
BUT SOMEONE NEEDS TO PICK A SUBJECT A LITTLE MORE UNDERSTANDABLE, LIKE A MOVIE TITLE OR TV SHOW.
EEK! THE BREAD'S BEEN STOLEN!
IS THAT WHAT YOU WERE TRYING TO TELL ME, SWAY? THAT I SHOULDN'T GET A SWOLLEN HEAD UNTIL I WAS FINISHED?

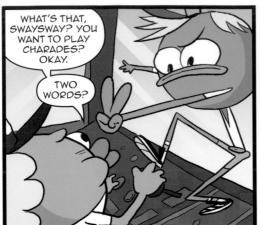

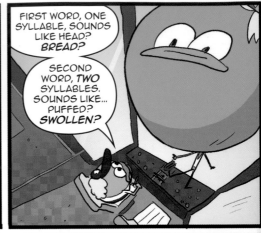

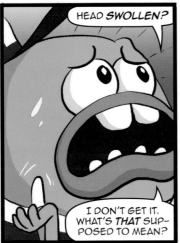

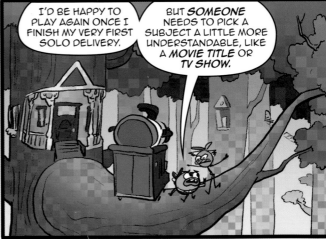

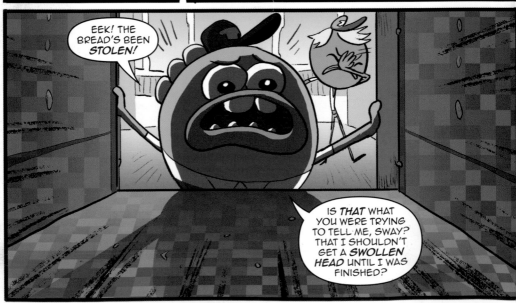

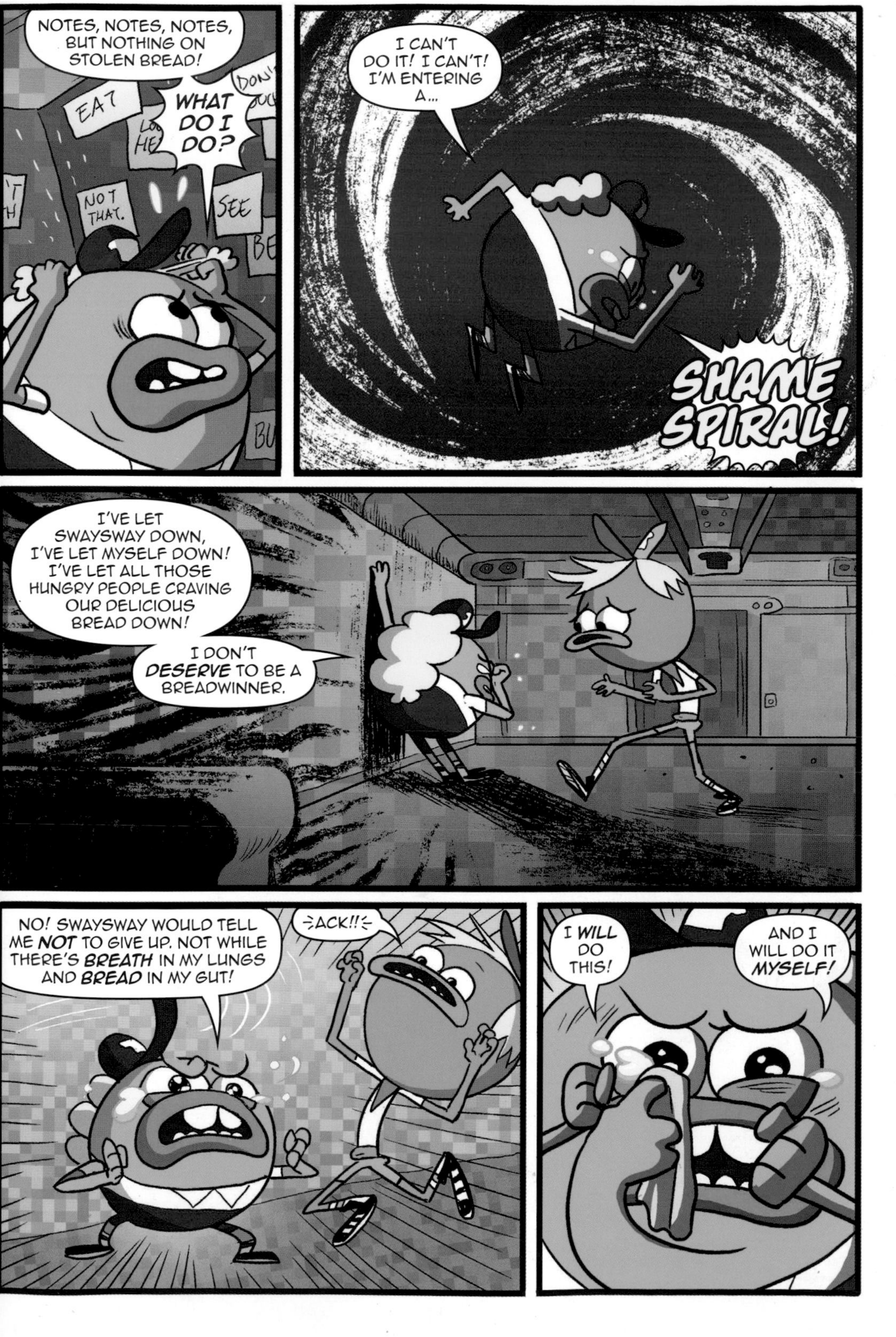
NOTES, NOTES, NOTES, BUT NOTHING ON STOLEN BREAD!
WHAT DO I DO?
EAT
NOT THAT.
SEE
I CAN'T DO IT! I CAN'T! I'M ENTERING A...
SHAME SPIRAL!
I'VE LET SWAYSWAY DOWN, I'VE LET MYSELF DOWN! I'VE LET ALL THOSE HUNGRY PEOPLE CRAVING OUR DELICIOUS BREAD DOWN!
I DON'T DESERVE TO BE A BREADWINNER.
NO! SWAYSWAY WOULD TELL ME NOT TO GIVE UP. NOT WHILE THERE'S BREATH IN MY LUNGS AND BREAD IN MY GUT!
ACK!!
I WILL DO THIS!
AND I WILL DO IT MYSELF!

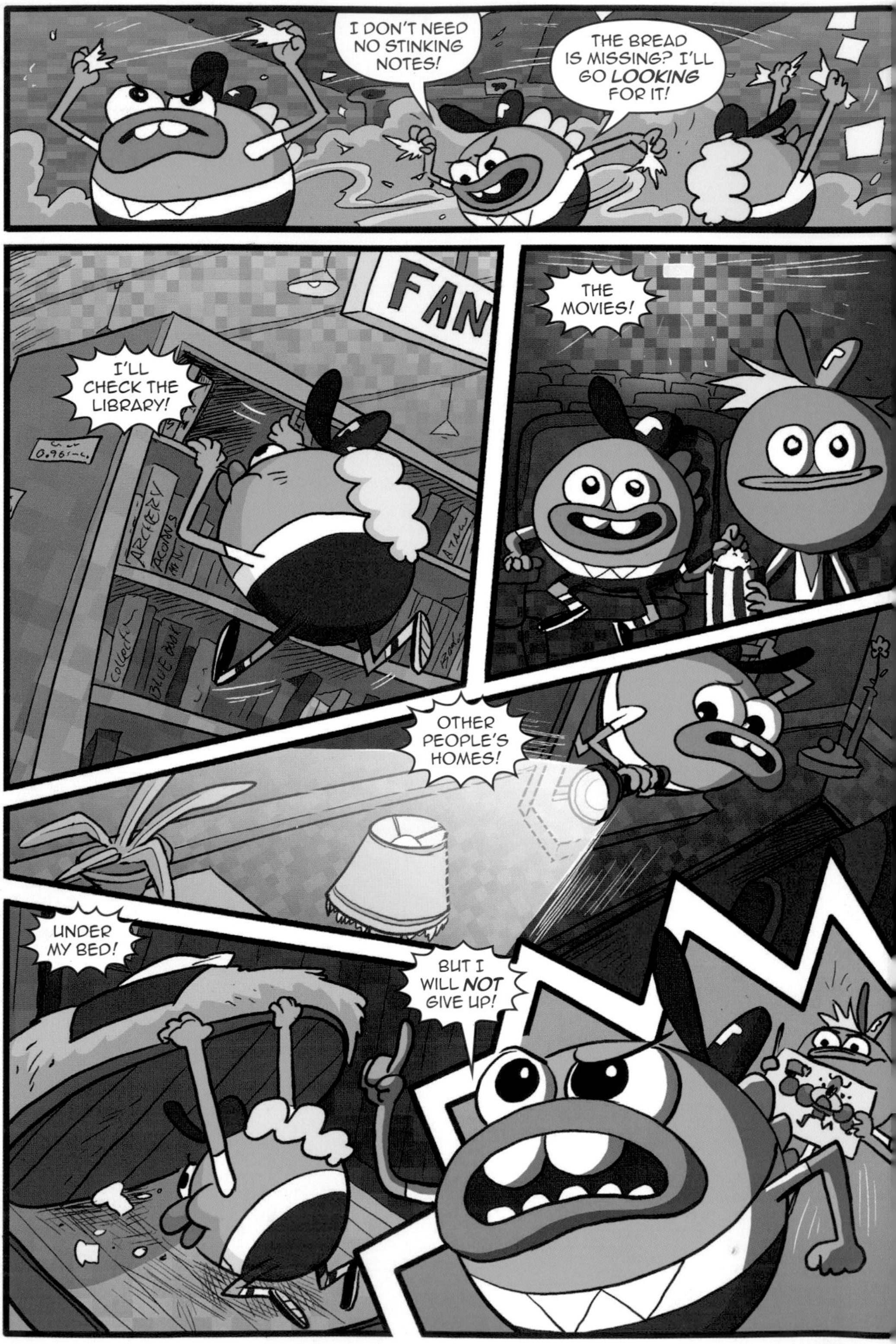
I DON'T NEED NO STINKING NOTES!
THE BREAD IS MISSING? I'LL GO LOOKING FOR IT!
FAN
I'LL CHECK THE LIBRARY!
ARCHERY
BLUE BOOK
THE MOVIES!
OTHER PEOPLE'S HOMES!
UNDER MY BED!
BUT I WILL NOT GIVE UP!

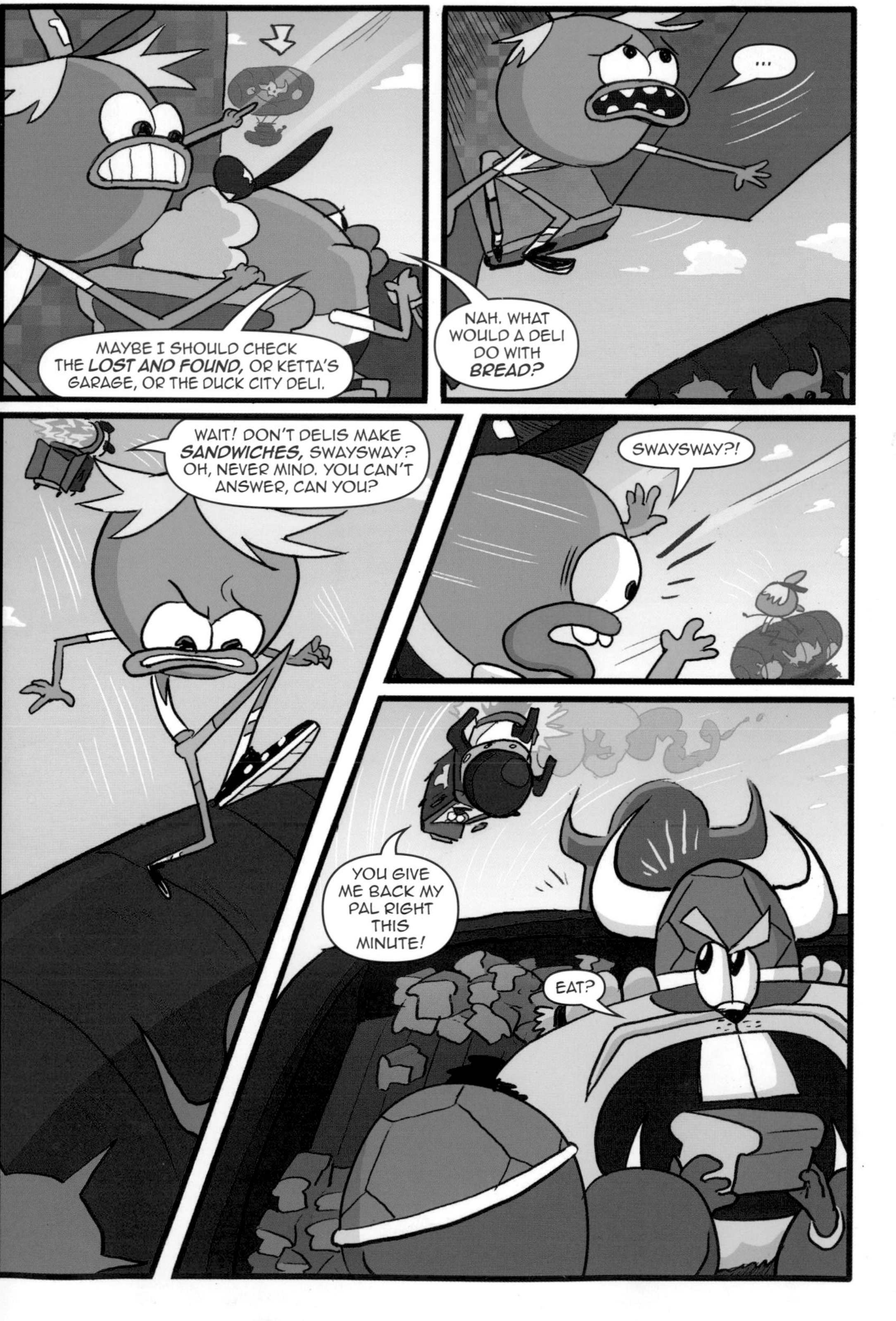
MAYBE I SHOULD CHECK THE LOST AND FOUND, OR KETTA'S GARAGE, OR THE DUCK CITY DELI.
...
NAH. WHAT WOULD A DELI DO WITH BREAD?
WAIT! DON'T DELIS MAKE SANDWICHES, SWAYSWAY? OH, NEVER MIND. YOU CAN'T ANSWER, CAN YOU?
SWAYSWAY?!
YOU GIVE ME BACK MY PAL RIGHT THIS MINUTE!
EAT?

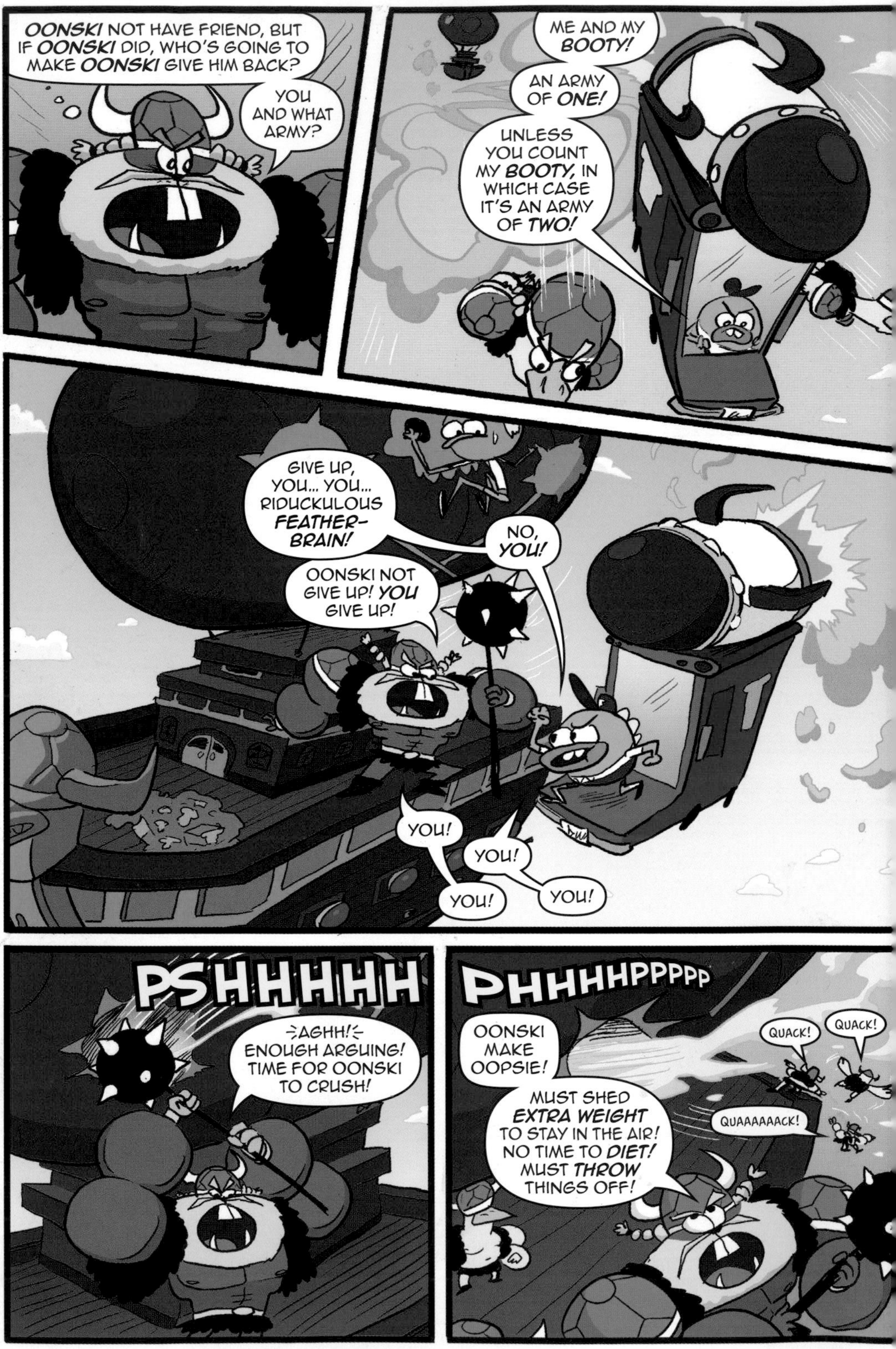
OONSKI NOT HAVE FRIEND, BUT IF OONSKI DID, WHO'S GOING TO MAKE OONSKI GIVE HIM BACK?
YOU AND WHAT ARMY?
ME AND MY BOOTY!
AN ARMY OF ONE!
UNLESS YOU COUNT MY BOOTY, IN WHICH CASE IT'S AN ARMY OF TWO!
GIVE UP, YOU... YOU... RIDUCKULOUS FEATHER-BRAIN!
NO, YOU!
OONSKI NOT GIVE UP! YOU GIVE UP!
YOU!
YOU!
YOU!
YOU!
PSHHHHHH
AGHH!
ENOUGH ARGUING! TIME FOR OONSKI TO CRUSH!
PHHHHPPPPP
OONSKI MAKE OOPSIE!
MUST SHED EXTRA WEIGHT TO STAY IN THE AIR! NO TIME TO DIET! MUST THROW THINGS OFF!
QUACK!
QUACK!
QUAAAAAACK!

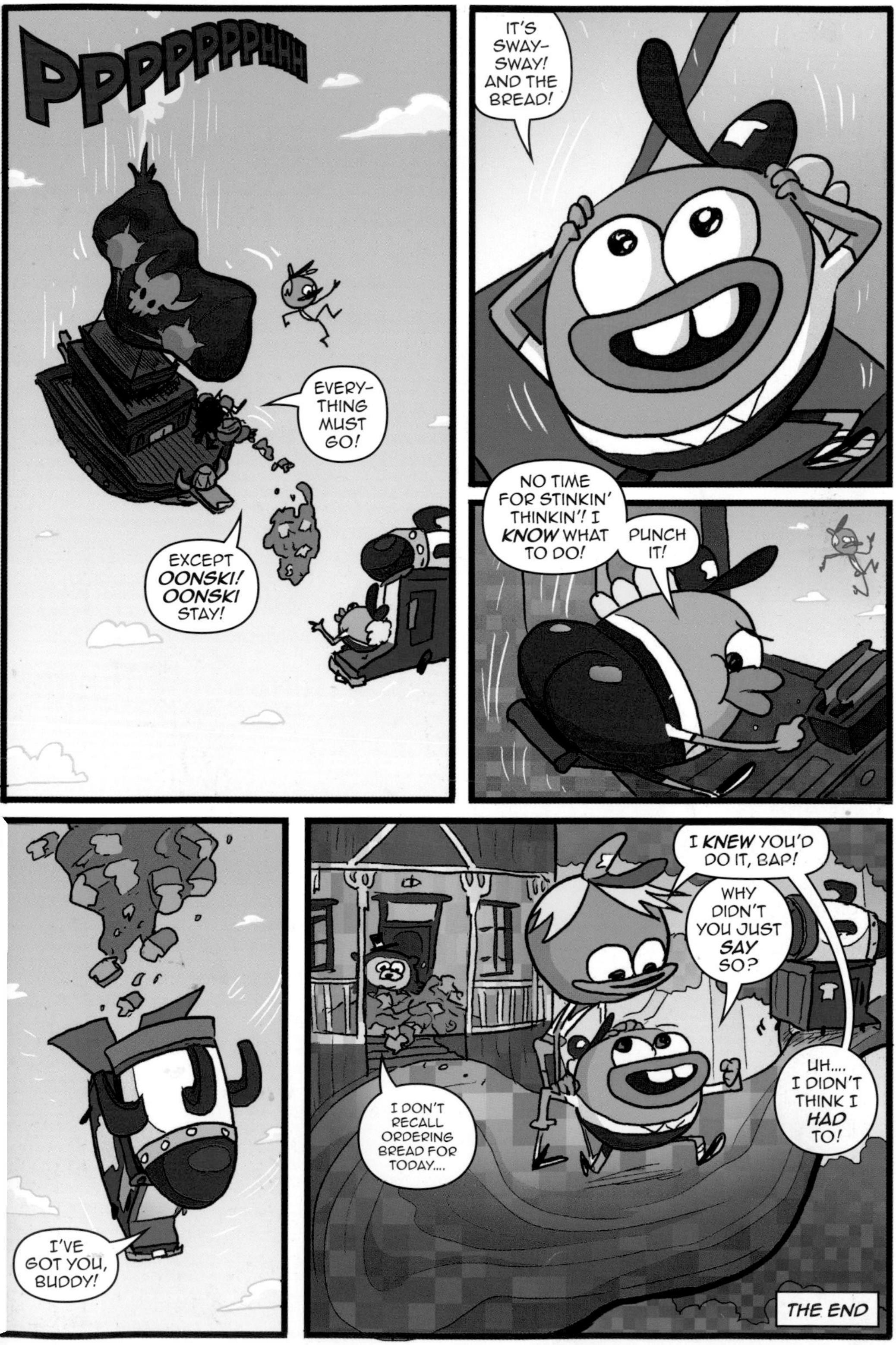
PPPPPPPHHH
EVERY-THING MUST GO!
EXCEPT OONSKI! OONSKI STAY!
IT'S SWAY-SWAY! AND THE BREAD!
NO TIME FOR STINKIN' THINKIN'! I KNOW WHAT TO DO!
PUNCH IT!
I'VE GOT YOU, BUDDY!
I KNEW YOU'D DO IT, BAP!
WHY DIDN'T YOU JUST SAY SO?
UH.... I DIDN'T THINK I HAD TO!
I DON'T RECALL ORDERING BREAD FOR TODAY....
THE END

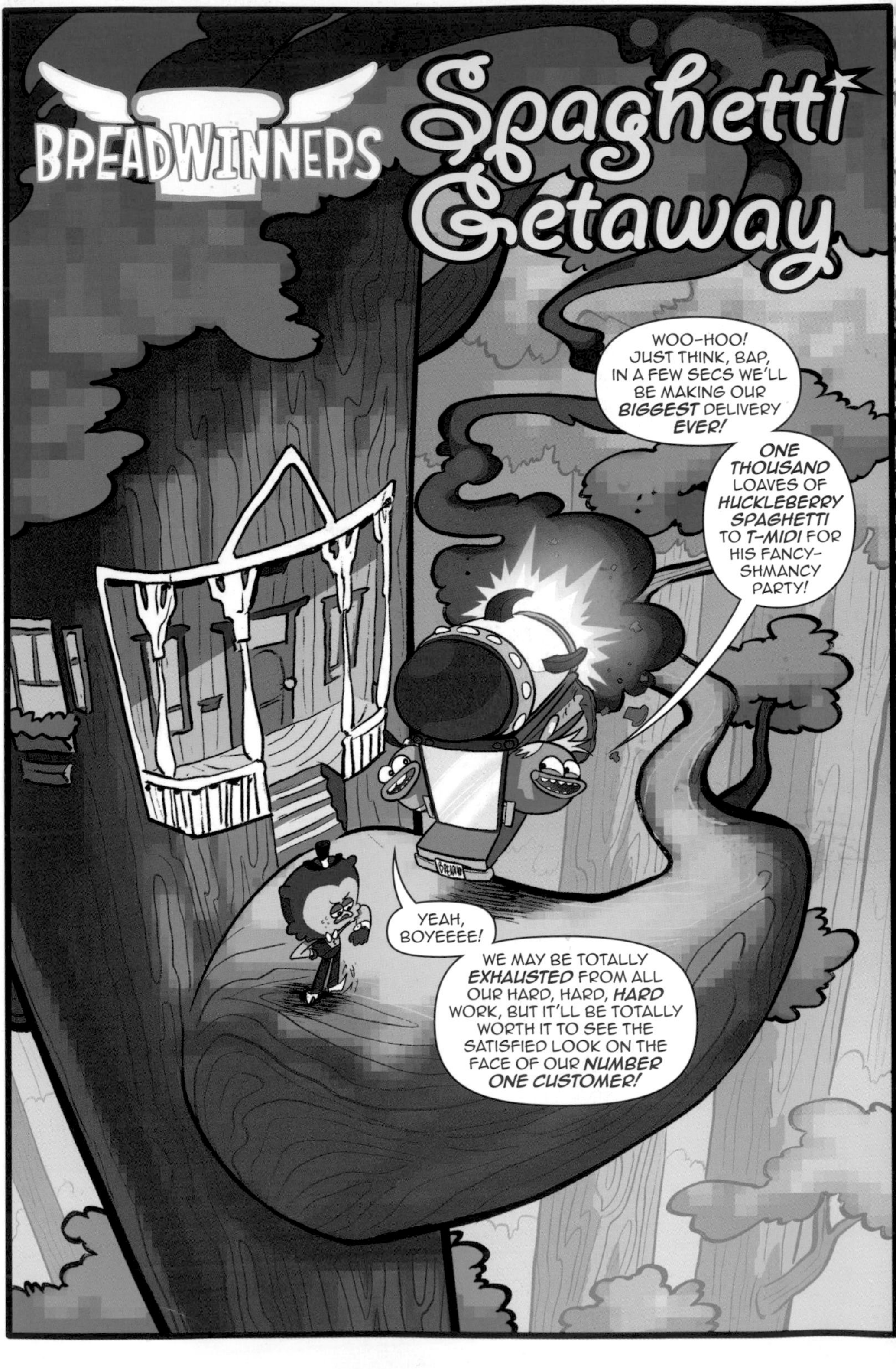
BREADWINNERS
Spaghetti Getaway
WOO-HOO! JUST THINK, BAP, IN A FEW SECS WE'LL BE MAKING OUR BIGGEST DELIVERY EVER!
ONE THOUSAND LOAVES OF HUCKLEBERRY SPAGHETTI TO T-MIDI FOR HIS FANCY-SHMANCY PARTY!
YEAH, BOYEEEE!
WE MAY BE TOTALLY EXHAUSTED FROM ALL OUR HARD, HARD, HARD WORK, BUT IT'LL BE TOTALLY WORTH IT TO SEE THE SATISFIED LOOK ON THE FACE OF OUR NUMBER ONE CUSTOMER!

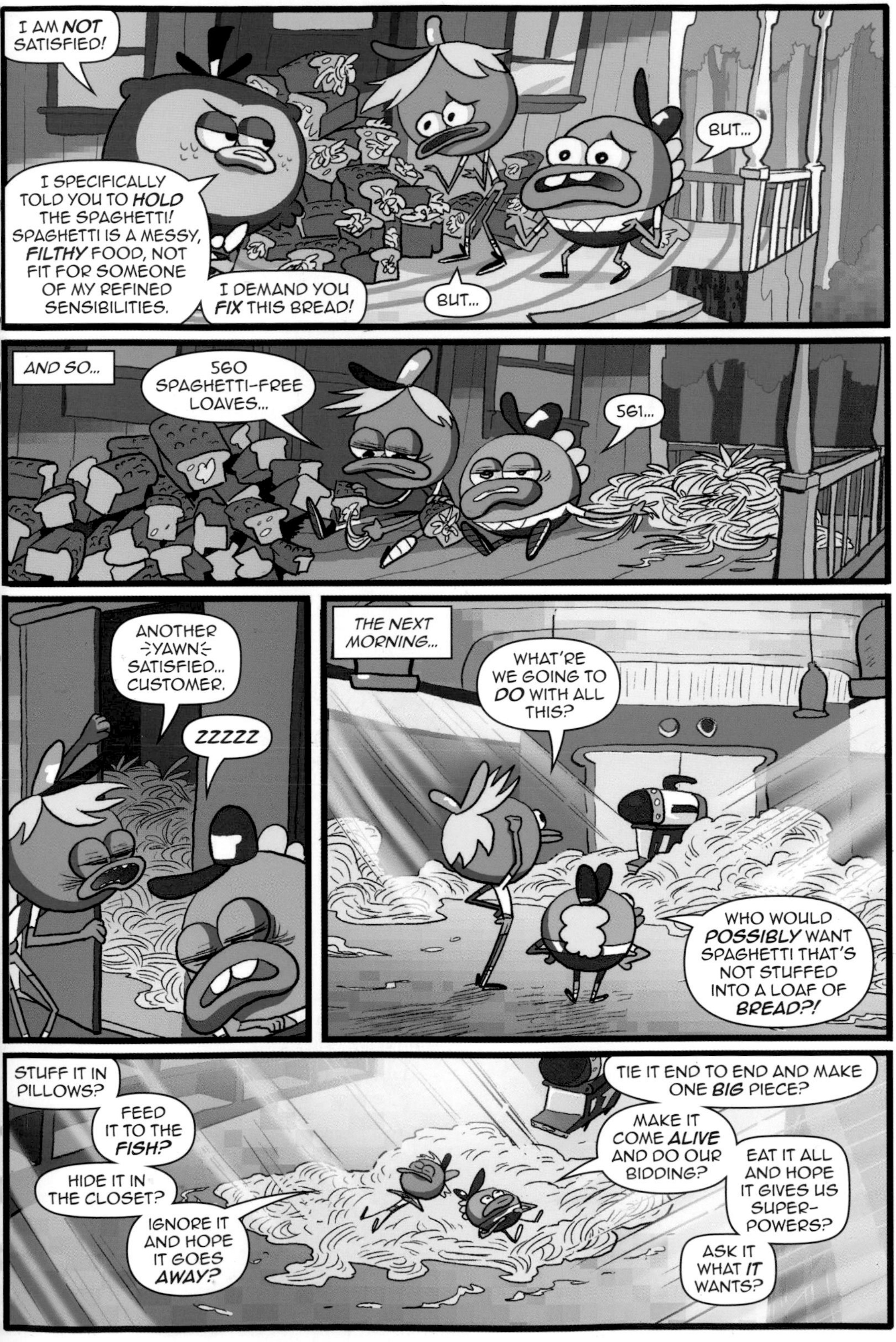

I AM NOT SATISFIED!
I SPECIFICALLY TOLD YOU TO HOLD THE SPAGHETTI! SPAGHETTI IS A MESSY, FILTHY FOOD, NOT FIT FOR SOMEONE OF MY REFINED SENSIBILITIES.
I DEMAND YOU FIX THIS BREAD!
BUT...
BUT...
AND SO...
560 SPAGHETTI-FREE LOAVES...
561...
ANOTHER ≈YAWN≈ SATISFIED... CUSTOMER.
ZZZZZ
THE NEXT MORNING...
WHAT'RE WE GOING TO DO WITH ALL THIS?
WHO WOULD POSSIBLY WANT SPAGHETTI THAT'S NOT STUFFED INTO A LOAF OF BREAD?!
STUFF IT IN PILLOWS?
FEED IT TO THE FISH?
HIDE IT IN THE CLOSET?
IGNORE IT AND HOPE IT GOES AWAY?
TIE IT END TO END AND MAKE ONE BIG PIECE?
MAKE IT COME ALIVE AND DO OUR BIDDING?
EAT IT ALL AND HOPE IT GIVES US SUPER-POWERS?
ASK IT WHAT IT WANTS?

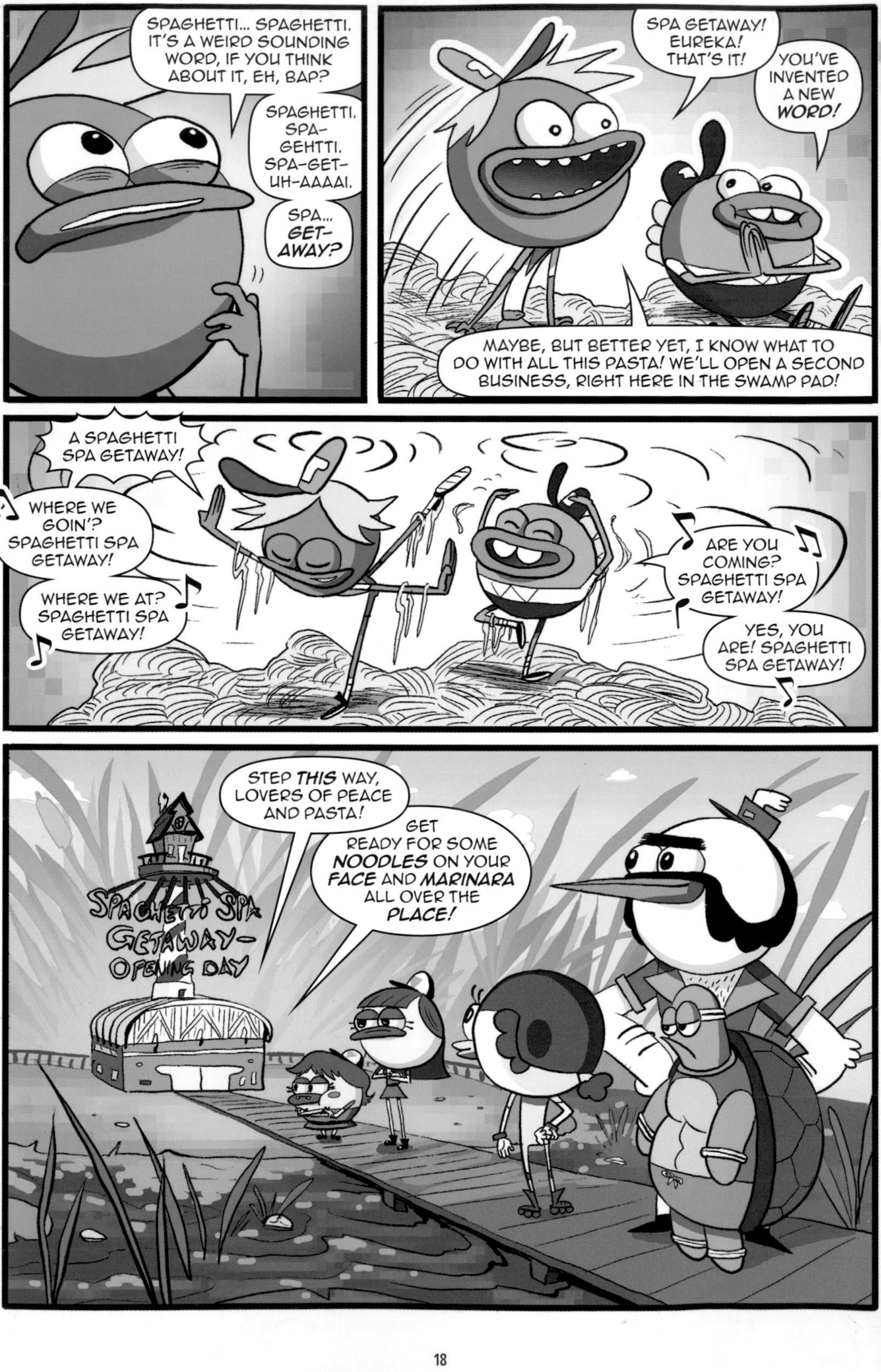
SPAGHETTI... SPAGHETTI. IT'S A WEIRD SOUNDING WORD, IF YOU THINK ABOUT IT, EH, BAP?
SPAGHETTI. SPA-GEHTTI. SPA-GET-UH-AAAAI.
SPA... GET-AWAY?
SPA GETAWAY! EUREKA! THAT'S IT!
YOU'VE INVENTED A NEW WORD!
MAYBE, BUT BETTER YET, I KNOW WHAT TO DO WITH ALL THIS PASTA! WE'LL OPEN A SECOND BUSINESS, RIGHT HERE IN THE SWAMP PAD!
A SPAGHETTI SPA GETAWAY!
WHERE WE GOIN'? SPAGHETTI SPA GETAWAY!
WHERE WE AT? SPAGHETTI SPA GETAWAY!
ARE YOU COMING? SPAGHETTI SPA GETAWAY!
YES, YOU ARE! SPAGHETTI SPA GETAWAY!
SPAGHETTI SPA GETAWAY- OPENING DAY
STEP THIS WAY, LOVERS OF PEACE AND PASTA!
GET READY FOR SOME NOODLES ON YOUR FACE AND MARINARA ALL OVER THE PLACE!

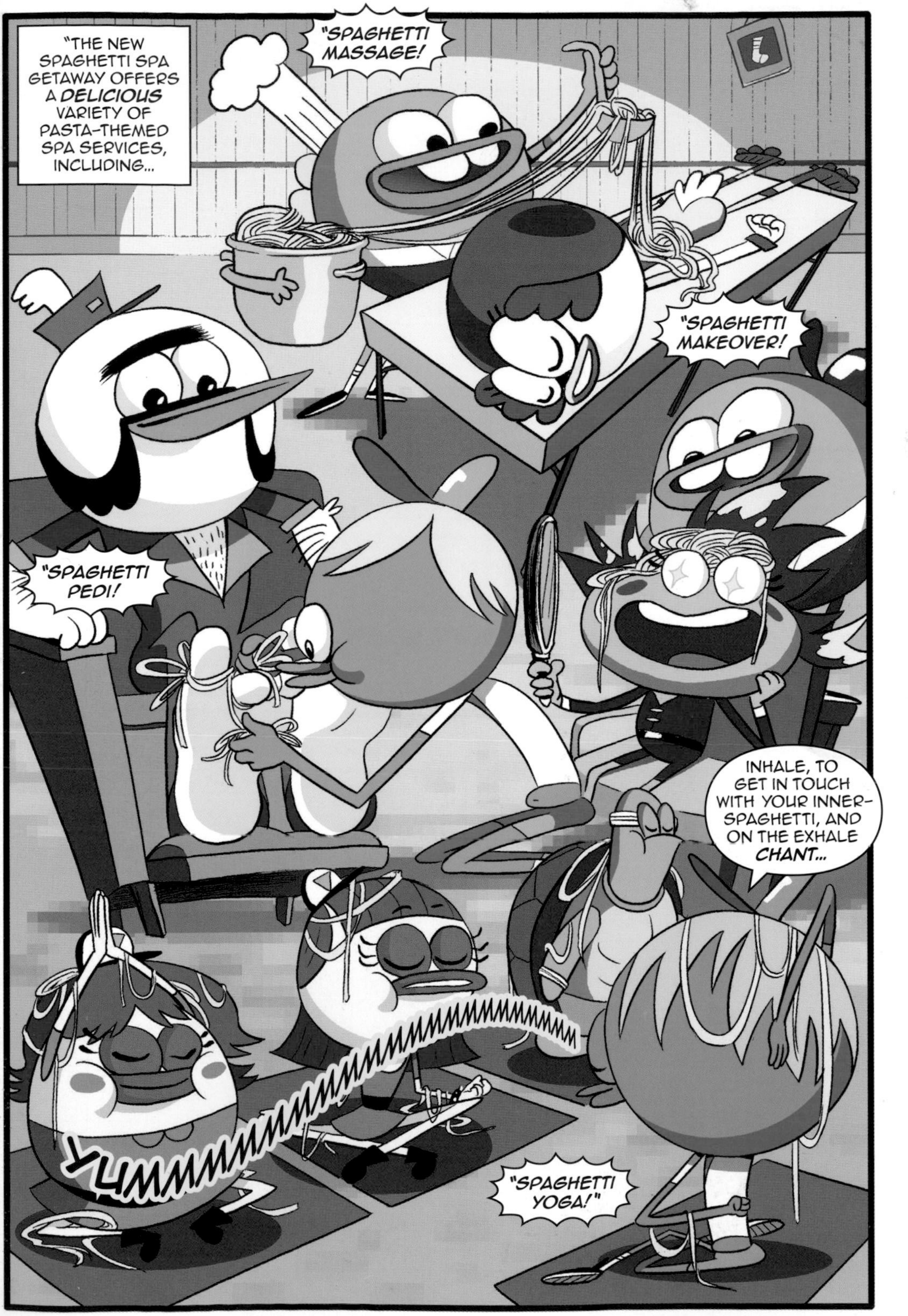
"THE NEW SPAGHETTI SPA GETAWAY OFFERS A DELICIOUS VARIETY OF PASTA-THEMED SPA SERVICES, INCLUDING...
"SPAGHETTI MASSAGE!
"SPAGHETTI MAKEOVER!
"SPAGHETTI PEDI!
INHALE, TO GET IN TOUCH WITH YOUR INNER-SPAGHETTI, AND ON THE EXHALE CHANT...
YUMMMMMMMMMMMMMMMMMMMMMMMMMMMMMMMMMM
"SPAGHETTI YOGA!"

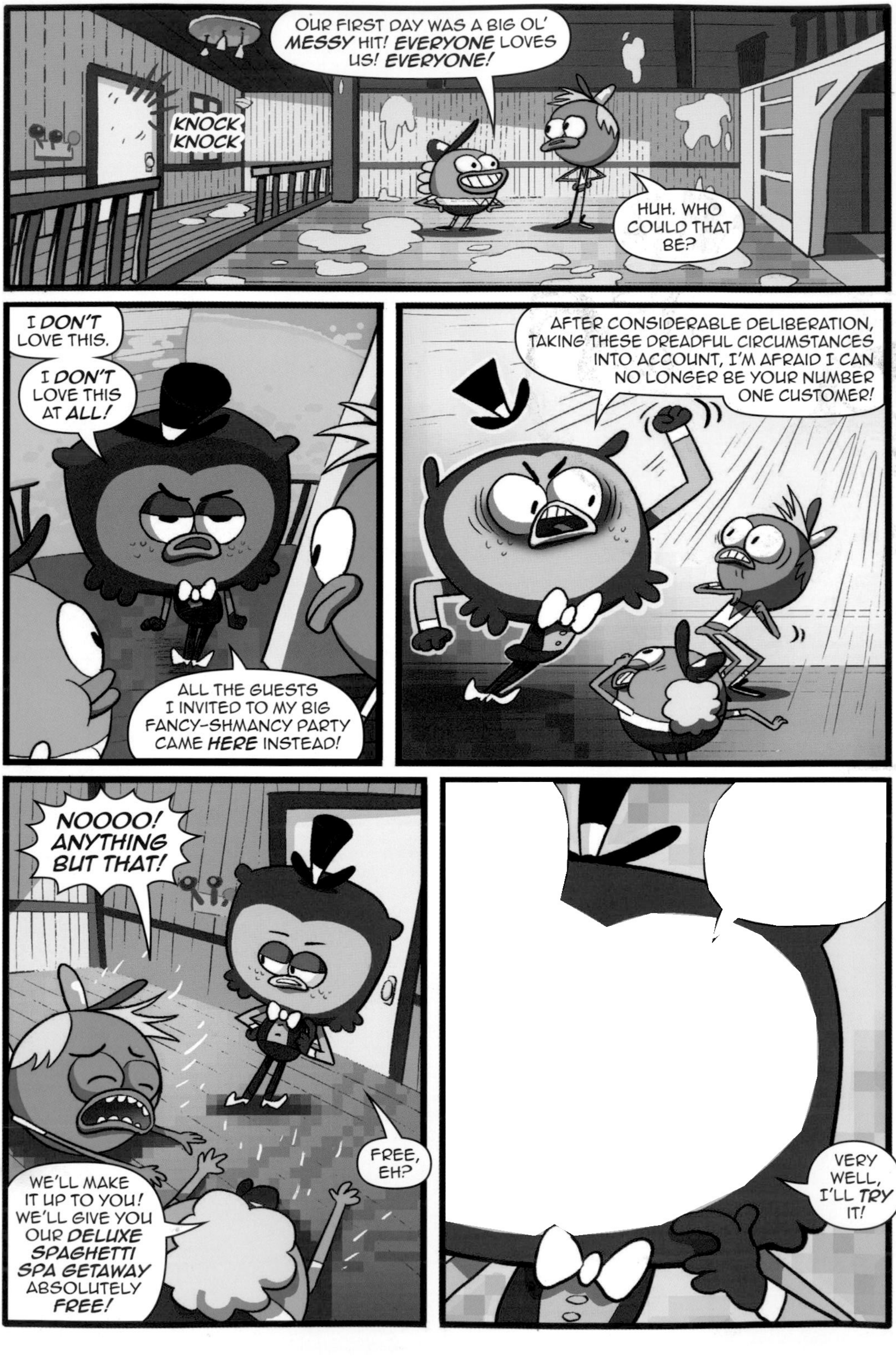
OUR FIRST DAY WAS A BIG OL' MESSY HIT! EVERYONE LOVES US! EVERYONE!
KNOCK KNOCK
HUH. WHO COULD THAT BE?
I DON'T LOVE THIS.
I DON'T LOVE THIS AT ALL!
ALL THE GUESTS I INVITED TO MY BIG FANCY-SHMANCY PARTY CAME HERE INSTEAD!
AFTER CONSIDERABLE DELIBERATION, TAKING THESE DREADFUL CIRCUMSTANCES INTO ACCOUNT, I'M AFRAID I CAN NO LONGER BE YOUR NUMBER ONE CUSTOMER!
NOOOO! ANYTHING BUT THAT!
WE'LL MAKE IT UP TO YOU! WE'LL GIVE YOU OUR DELUXE SPAGHETTI SPA GETAWAY ABSOLUTELY FREE!
FREE, EH?
VERY WELL, I'LL TRY IT!

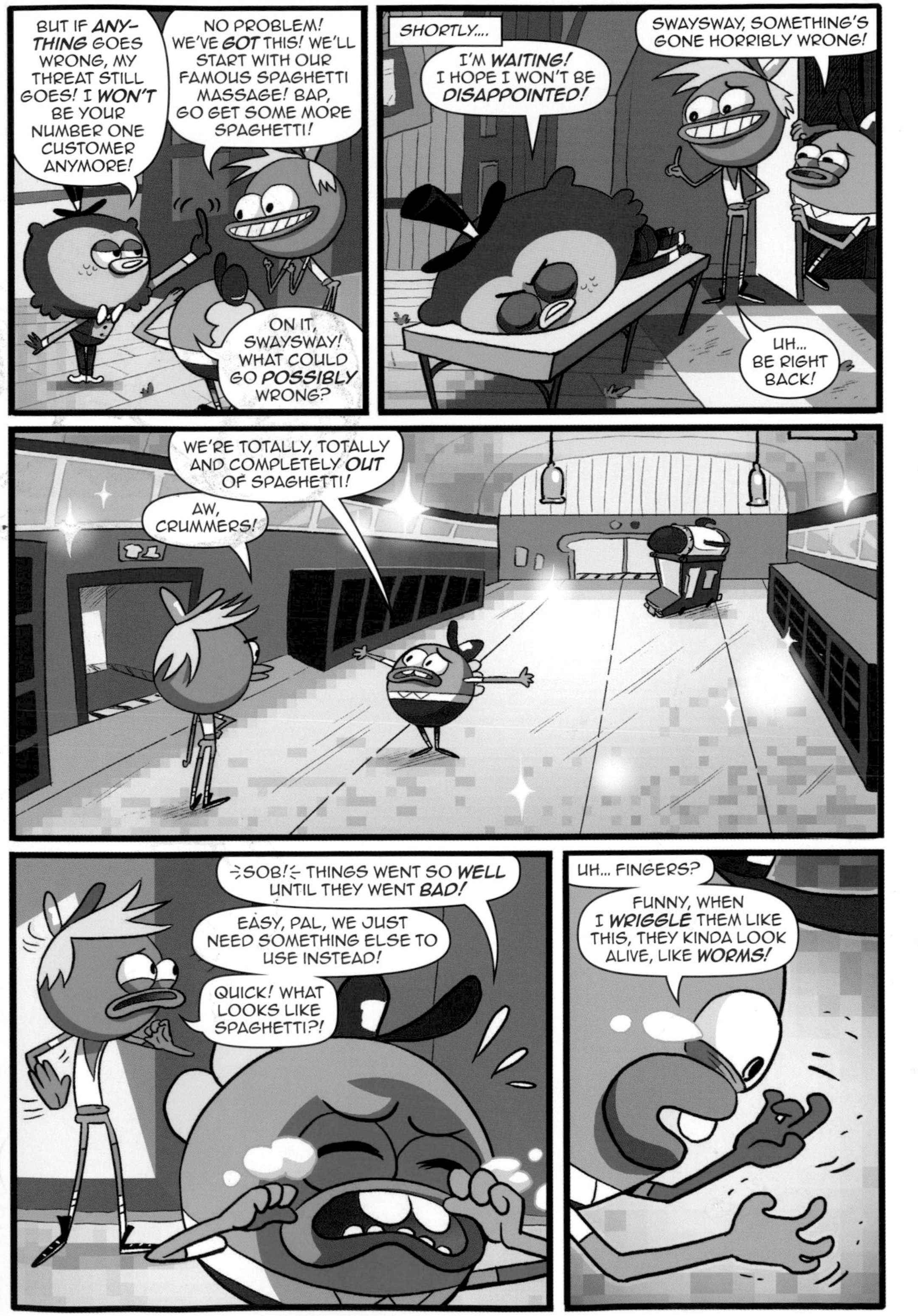
BUT IF ANY-THING GOES WRONG, MY THREAT STILL GOES! I WON'T BE YOUR NUMBER ONE CUSTOMER ANYMORE!
NO PROBLEM! WE'VE GOT THIS! WE'LL START WITH OUR FAMOUS SPAGHETTI MASSAGE! BAP, GO GET SOME MORE SPAGHETTI!
ON IT, SWAYSWAY! WHAT COULD GO POSSIBLY WRONG?
SHORTLY....
I'M WAITING! I HOPE I WON'T BE DISAPPOINTED!
SWAYSWAY, SOMETHING'S GONE HORRIBLY WRONG!
UH... BE RIGHT BACK!
WE'RE TOTALLY, TOTALLY AND COMPLETELY OUT OF SPAGHETTI!
AW, CRUMMERS!
SOB! THINGS WENT SO WELL UNTIL THEY WENT BAD!
EASY, PAL, WE JUST NEED SOMETHING ELSE TO USE INSTEAD!
QUICK! WHAT LOOKS LIKE SPAGHETTI?!
UH... FINGERS?
FUNNY, WHEN I WRIGGLE THEM LIKE THIS, THEY KINDA LOOK ALIVE, LIKE WORMS!

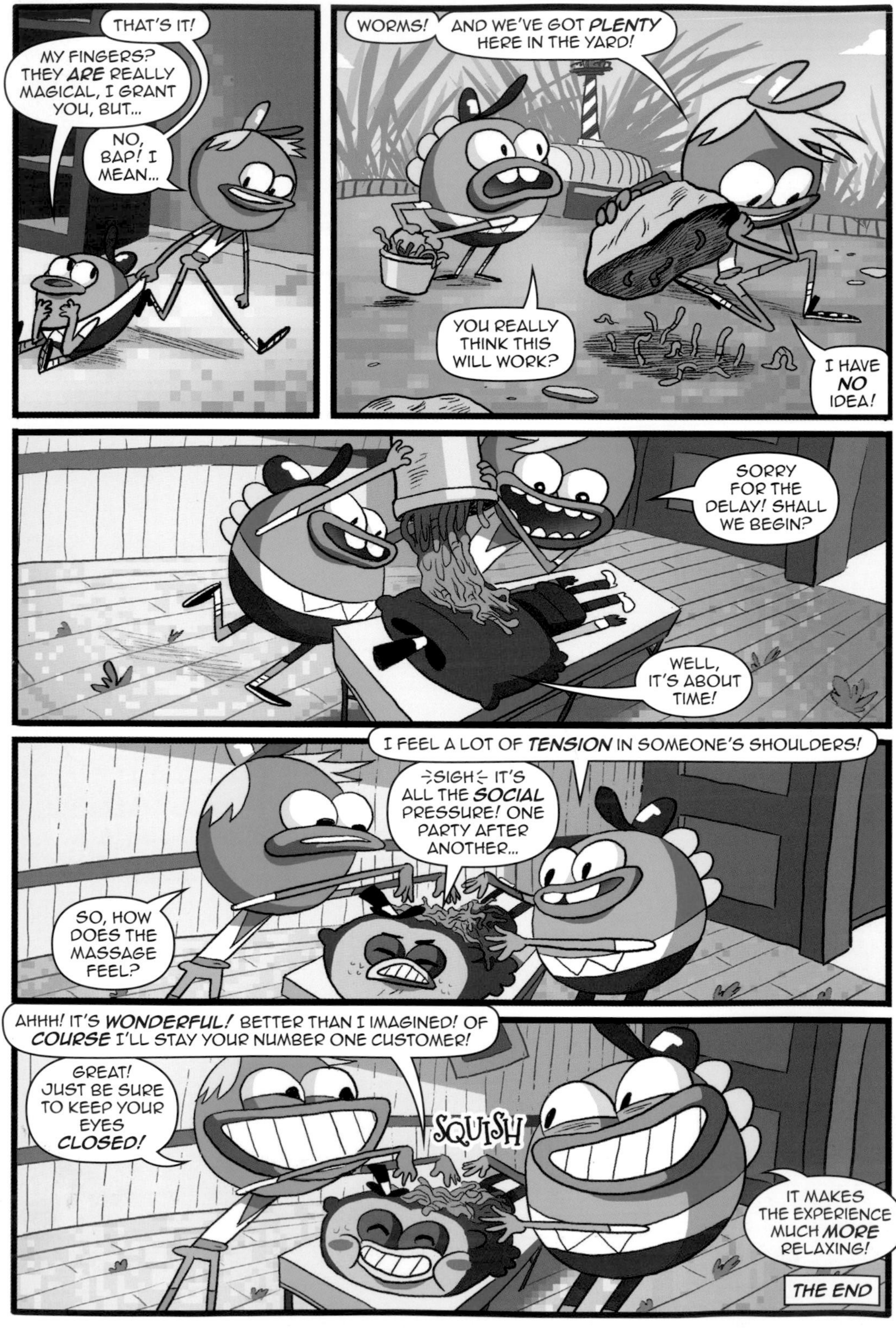
THAT'S IT!
MY FINGERS? THEY ARE REALLY MAGICAL, I GRANT YOU, BUT...
NO, BAP! I MEAN...
WORMS!
AND WE'VE GOT PLENTY HERE IN THE YARD!
YOU REALLY THINK THIS WILL WORK?
I HAVE NO IDEA!
SORRY FOR THE DELAY! SHALL WE BEGIN?
WELL, IT'S ABOUT TIME!
I FEEL A LOT OF TENSION IN SOMEONE'S SHOULDERS!
SIGH IT'S ALL THE SOCIAL PRESSURE! ONE PARTY AFTER ANOTHER...
SO, HOW DOES THE MASSAGE FEEL?
AHHH! IT'S WONDERFUL! BETTER THAN I IMAGINED! OF COURSE I'LL STAY YOUR NUMBER ONE CUSTOMER!
GREAT! JUST BE SURE TO KEEP YOUR EYES CLOSED!
SQUISH
IT MAKES THE EXPERIENCE MUCH MORE RELAXING!
THE END

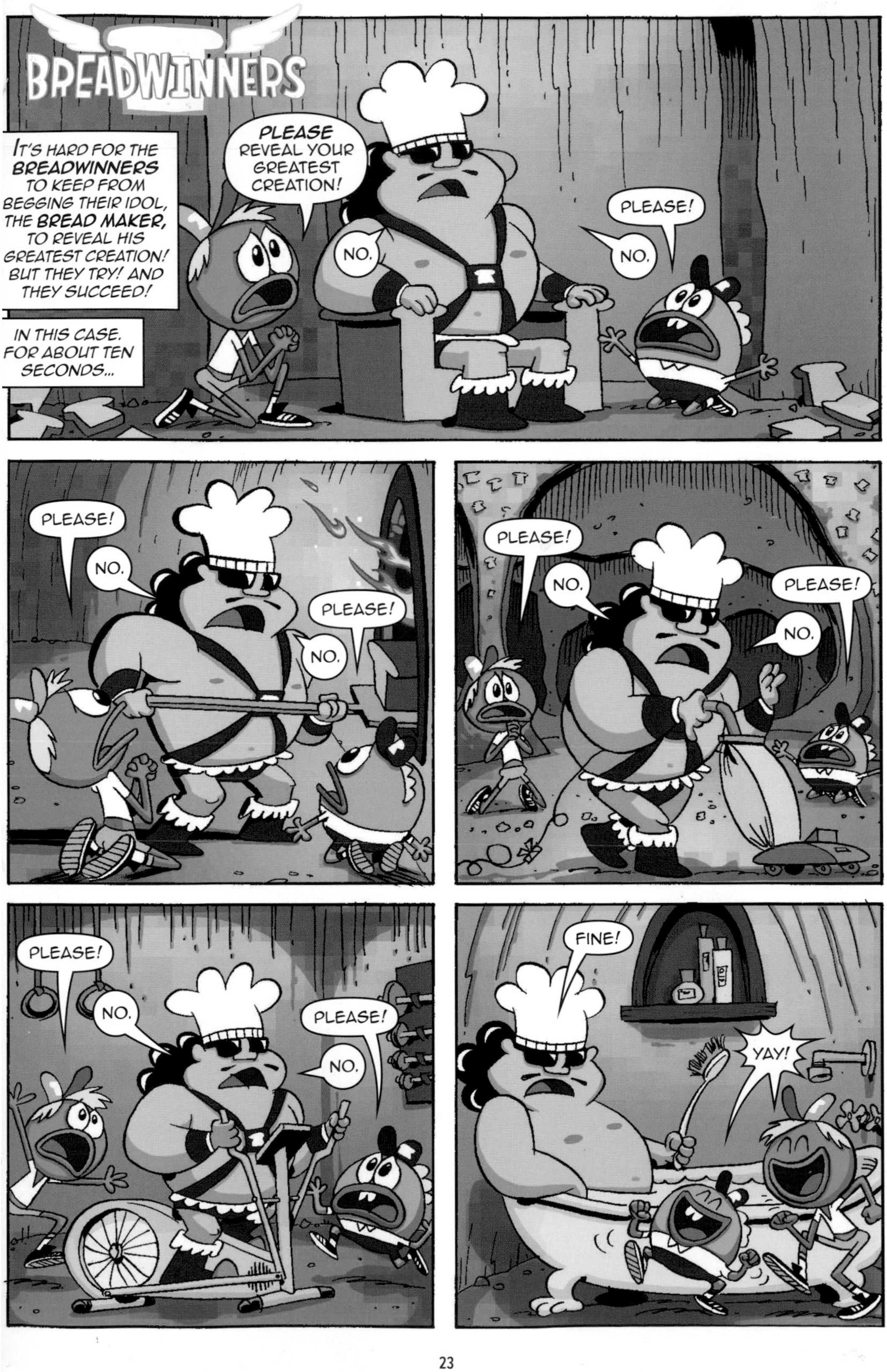

BREADWINNERS
IT'S HARD FOR THE BREADWINNERS TO KEEP FROM BEGGING THEIR IDOL, THE BREAD MAKER, TO REVEAL HIS GREATEST CREATION! BUT THEY TRY! AND THEY SUCCEED!
IN THIS CASE. FOR ABOUT TEN SECONDS...
PLEASE REVEAL YOUR GREATEST CREATION!
NO.
PLEASE!
NO.
PLEASE!
NO.
PLEASE!
NO.
PLEASE!
NO.
PLEASE!
NO.
PLEASE!
NO.
PLEASE!
NO.
FINE!
YAY!

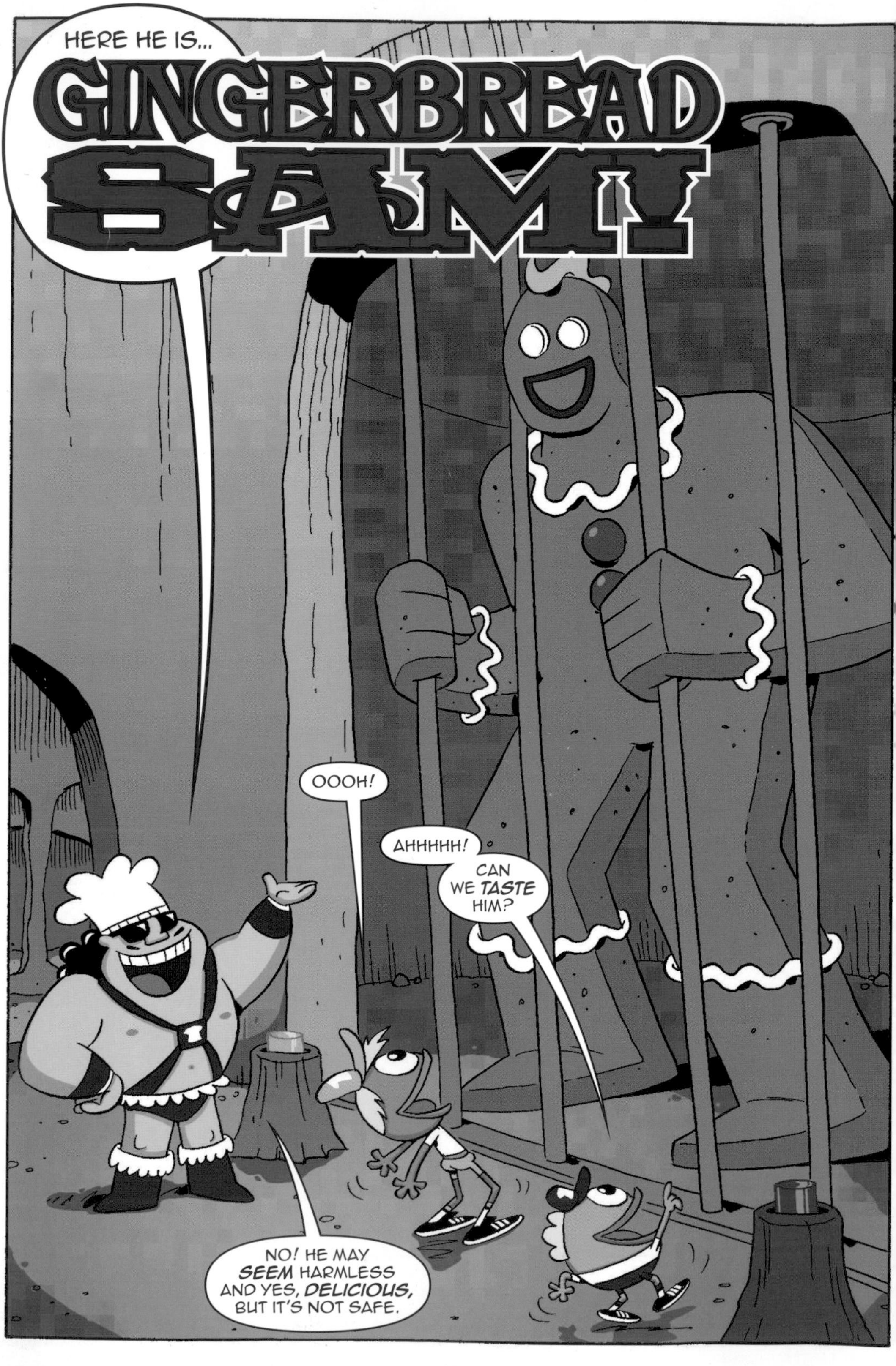
HERE HE IS...
GINGERBREAD SAMMY
OOOH!
AHHHHH!
CAN WE TASTE HIM?
NO! HE MAY SEEM HARMLESS AND YES, DELICIOUS, BUT IT'S NOT SAFE.

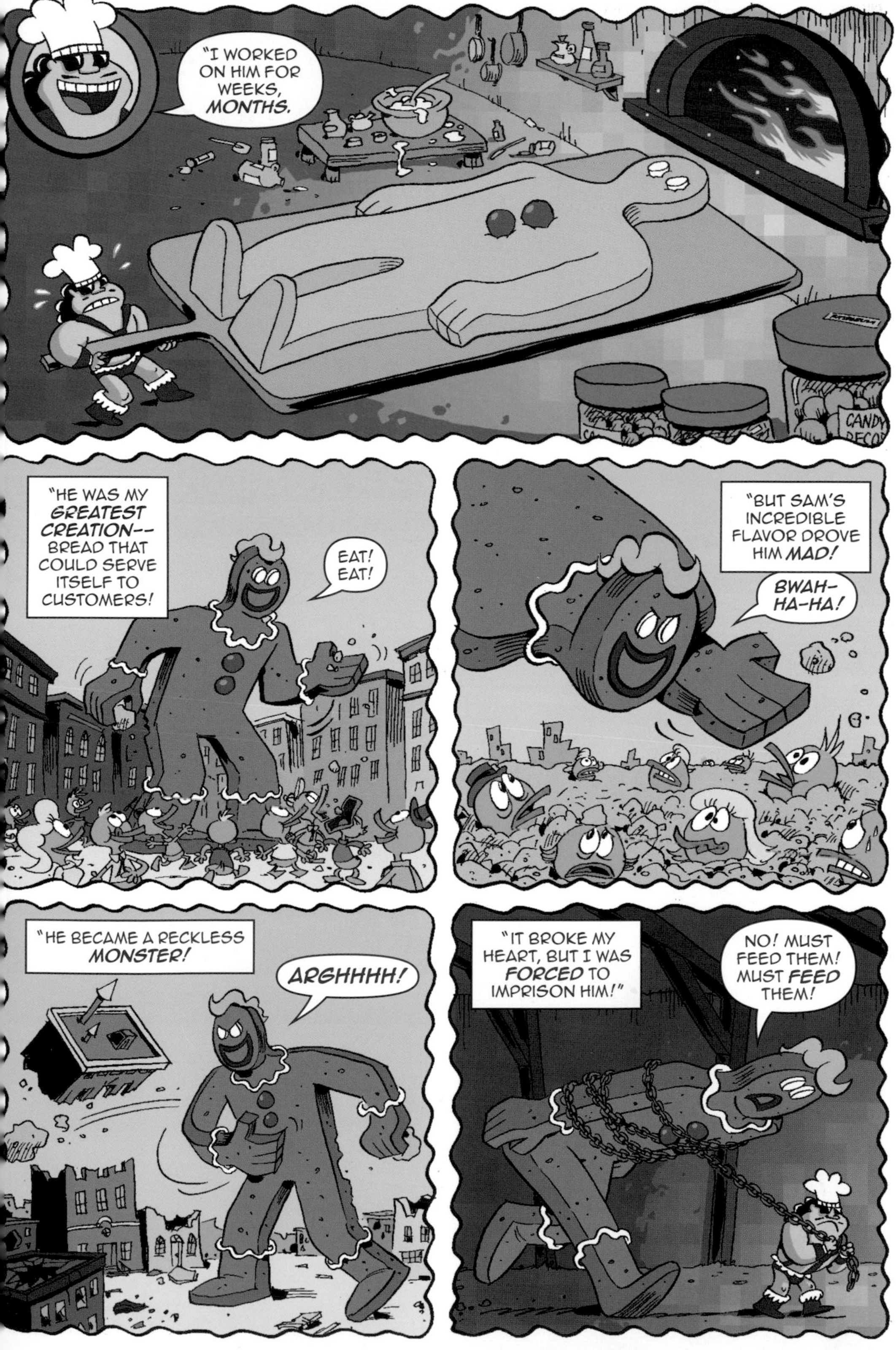
"I WORKED ON HIM FOR WEEKS, MONTHS.
CANDY DECOR
"HE WAS MY GREATEST CREATION-- BREAD THAT COULD SERVE ITSELF TO CUSTOMERS!
EAT! EAT!
"BUT SAM'S INCREDIBLE FLAVOR DROVE HIM MAD!
BWAH-HA-HA!
"HE BECAME A RECKLESS MONSTER!
ARGHHHH!
"IT BROKE MY HEART, BUT I WAS FORCED TO IMPRISON HIM!"
NO! MUST FEED THEM! MUST FEED THEM!

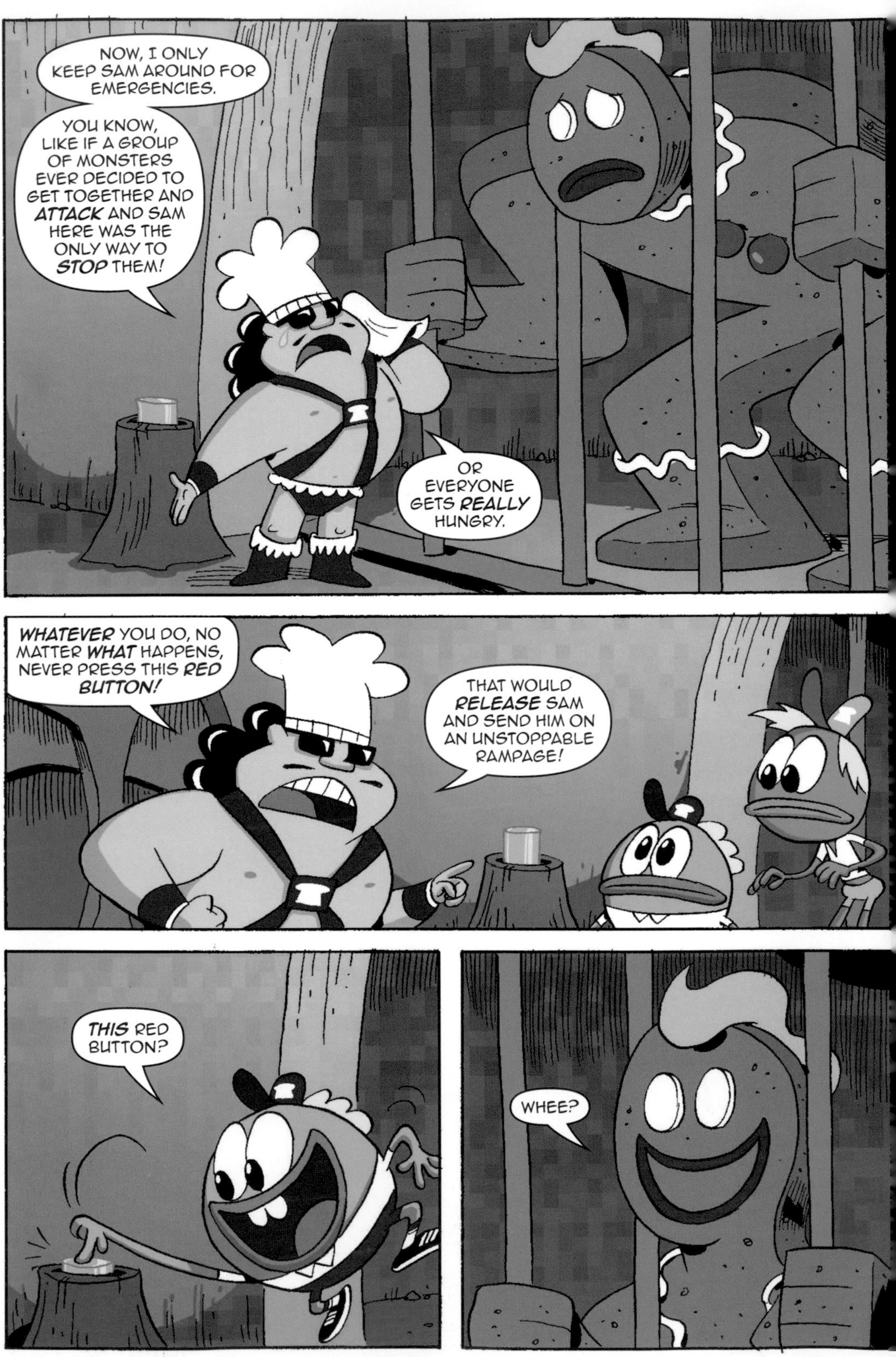
NOW, I ONLY KEEP SAM AROUND FOR EMERGENCIES.
YOU KNOW, LIKE IF A GROUP OF MONSTERS EVER DECIDED TO GET TOGETHER AND *ATTACK* AND SAM HERE WAS THE ONLY WAY TO *STOP* THEM!
OR EVERYONE GETS *REALLY* HUNGRY.
WHATEVER YOU DO, NO MATTER *WHAT* HAPPENS, NEVER PRESS THIS *RED BUTTON!*
THAT WOULD *RELEASE* SAM AND SEND HIM ON AN UNSTOPPABLE RAMPAGE!
THIS RED BUTTON?
WHEE?

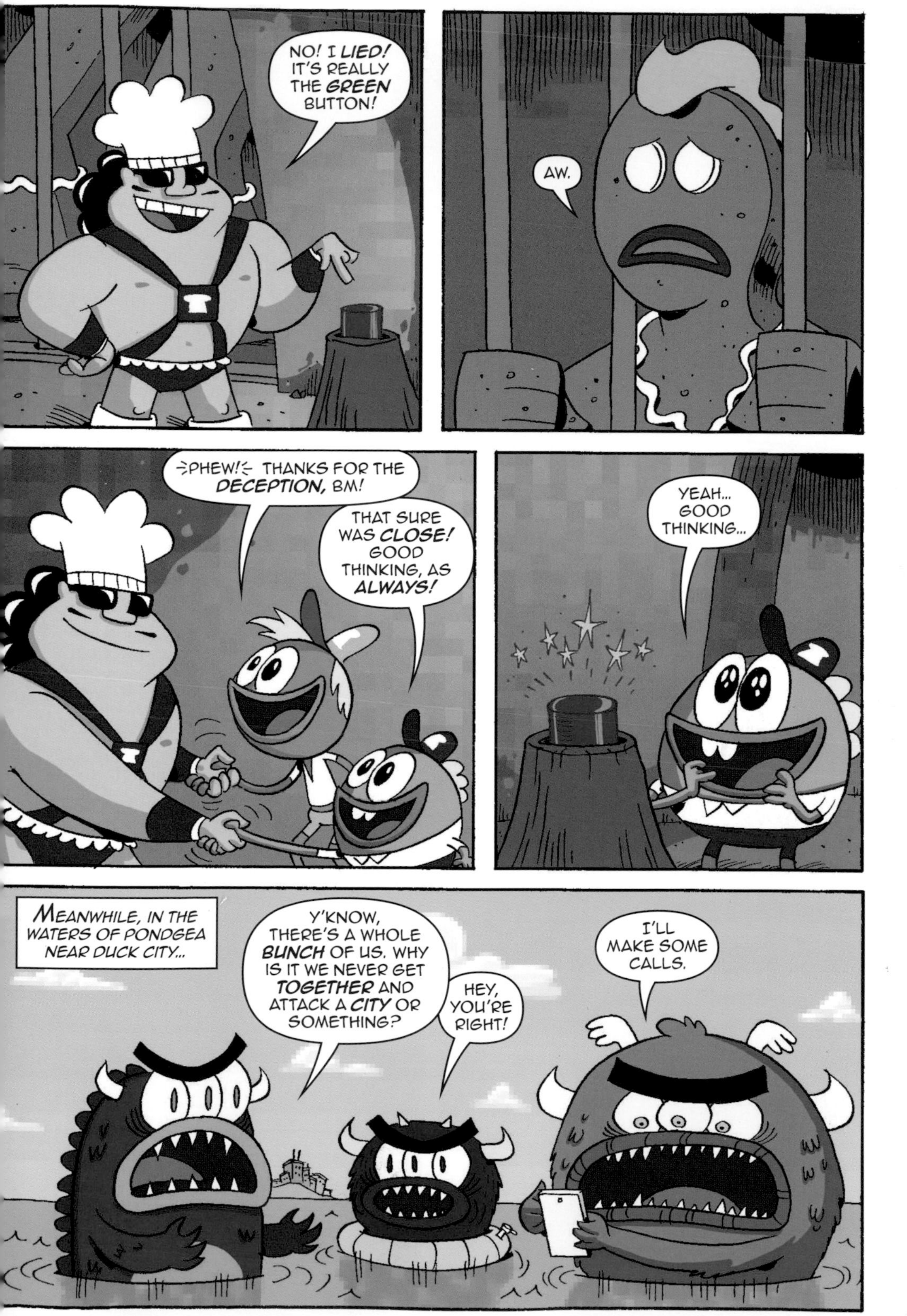
NO! I LIED! IT'S REALLY THE GREEN BUTTON!
AW.
PHEW! THANKS FOR THE DECEPTION, BM!
THAT SURE WAS CLOSE! GOOD THINKING, AS ALWAYS!
YEAH... GOOD THINKING...
MEANWHILE, IN THE WATERS OF PONDGEA NEAR DUCK CITY...
Y'KNOW, THERE'S A WHOLE BUNCH OF US. WHY IS IT WE NEVER GET TOGETHER AND ATTACK A CITY OR SOMETHING?
HEY, YOU'RE RIGHT!
I'LL MAKE SOME CALLS.

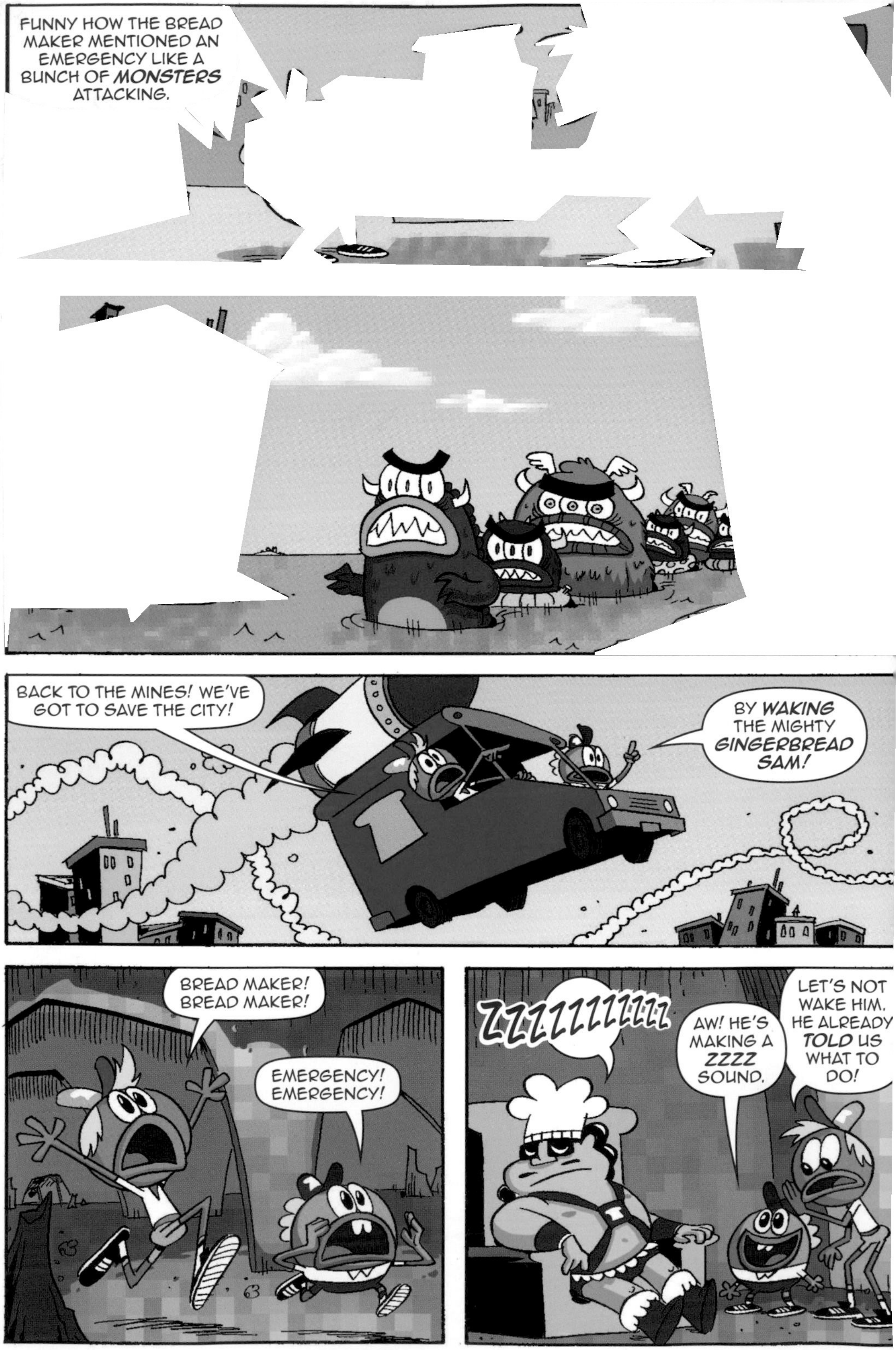

FUNNY HOW THE BREAD MAKER MENTIONED AN EMERGENCY LIKE A BUNCH OF MONSTERS ATTACKING.
BACK TO THE MINES! WE'VE GOT TO SAVE THE CITY!
BY WAKING THE MIGHTY GINGERBREAD SAM!
BREAD MAKER! BREAD MAKER!
EMERGENCY! EMERGENCY!
ZZZZZZZZZZZZZ
AW! HE'S MAKING A ZZZZ SOUND.
LET'S NOT WAKE HIM. HE ALREADY TOLD US WHAT TO DO!

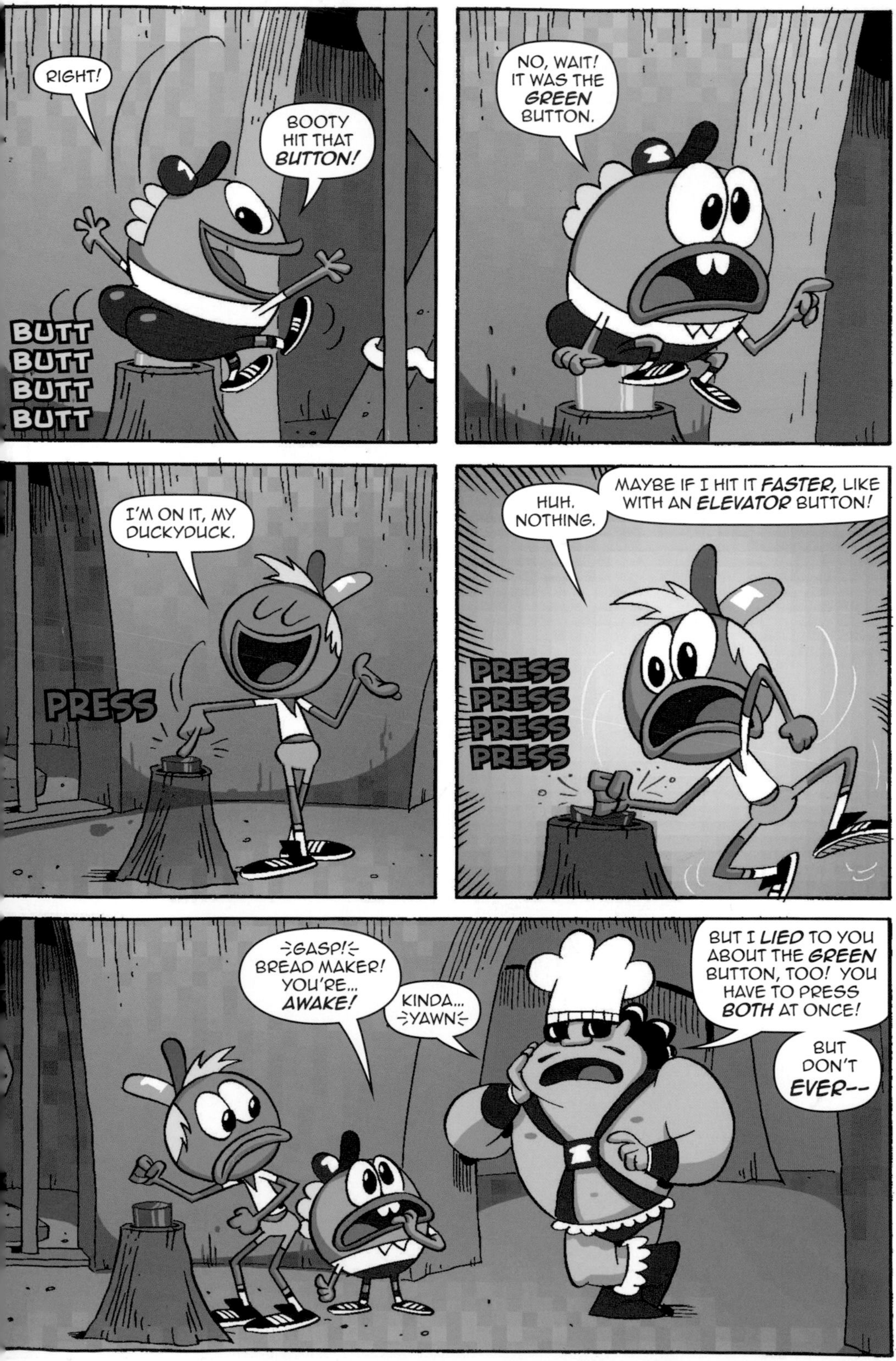
RIGHT!
BOOTY HIT THAT BUTTON!
BUTT BUTT BUTT BUTT
NO, WAIT! IT WAS THE GREEN BUTTON.
I'M ON IT, MY DUCKYDUCK.
PRESS
HUH. NOTHING.
MAYBE IF I HIT IT FASTER, LIKE WITH AN ELEVATOR BUTTON!
PRESS PRESS PRESS PRESS
GASP! BREAD MAKER! YOU'RE... AWAKE!
KINDA... YAWN
BUT I LIED TO YOU ABOUT THE GREEN BUTTON, TOO! YOU HAVE TO PRESS BOTH AT ONCE!
BUT DON'T EVER--

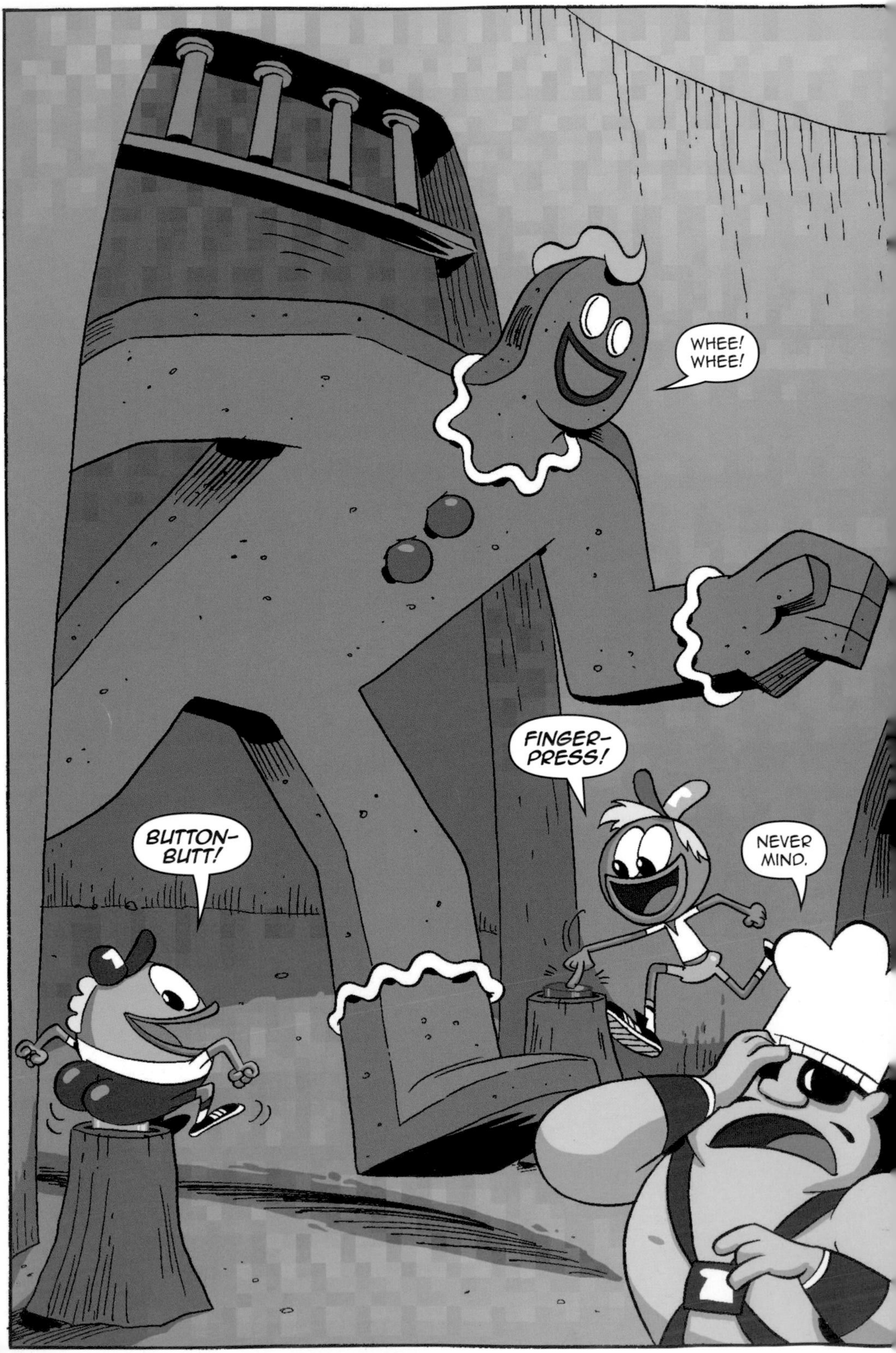
WHEE! WHEE!
FINGER-PRESS!
BUTTON-BUTT!
NEVER MIND.

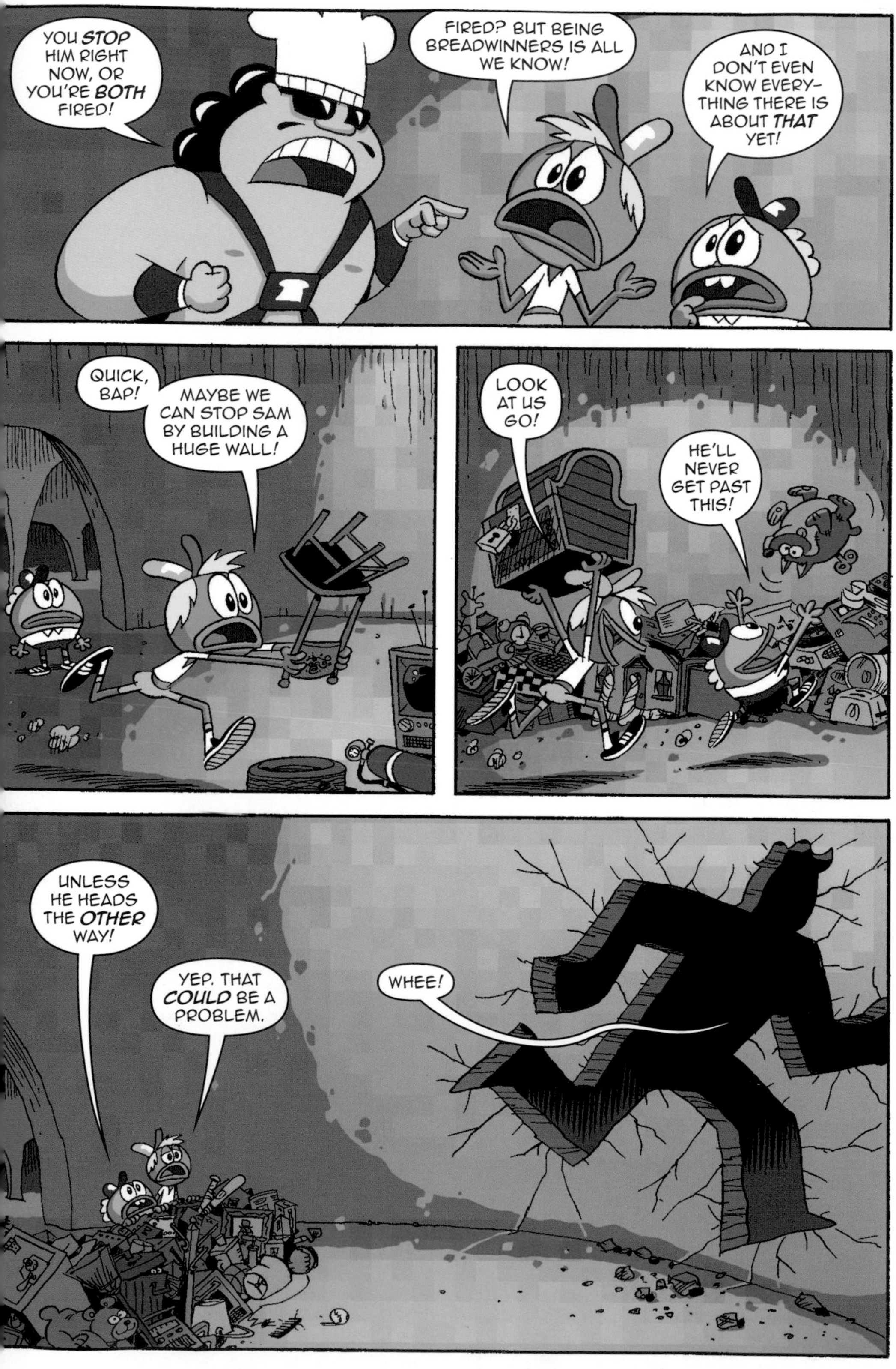
YOU *STOP* HIM RIGHT NOW, OR YOU'RE *BOTH* FIRED!
FIRED? BUT BEING BREADWINNERS IS ALL WE KNOW!
AND I DON'T EVEN KNOW EVERY-THING THERE IS ABOUT *THAT* YET!
QUICK, BAP!
MAYBE WE CAN STOP SAM BY BUILDING A HUGE WALL!
LOOK AT US GO!
HE'LL NEVER GET PAST THIS!
UNLESS HE HEADS THE *OTHER* WAY!
YEP. THAT *COULD* BE A PROBLEM.
WHEE!

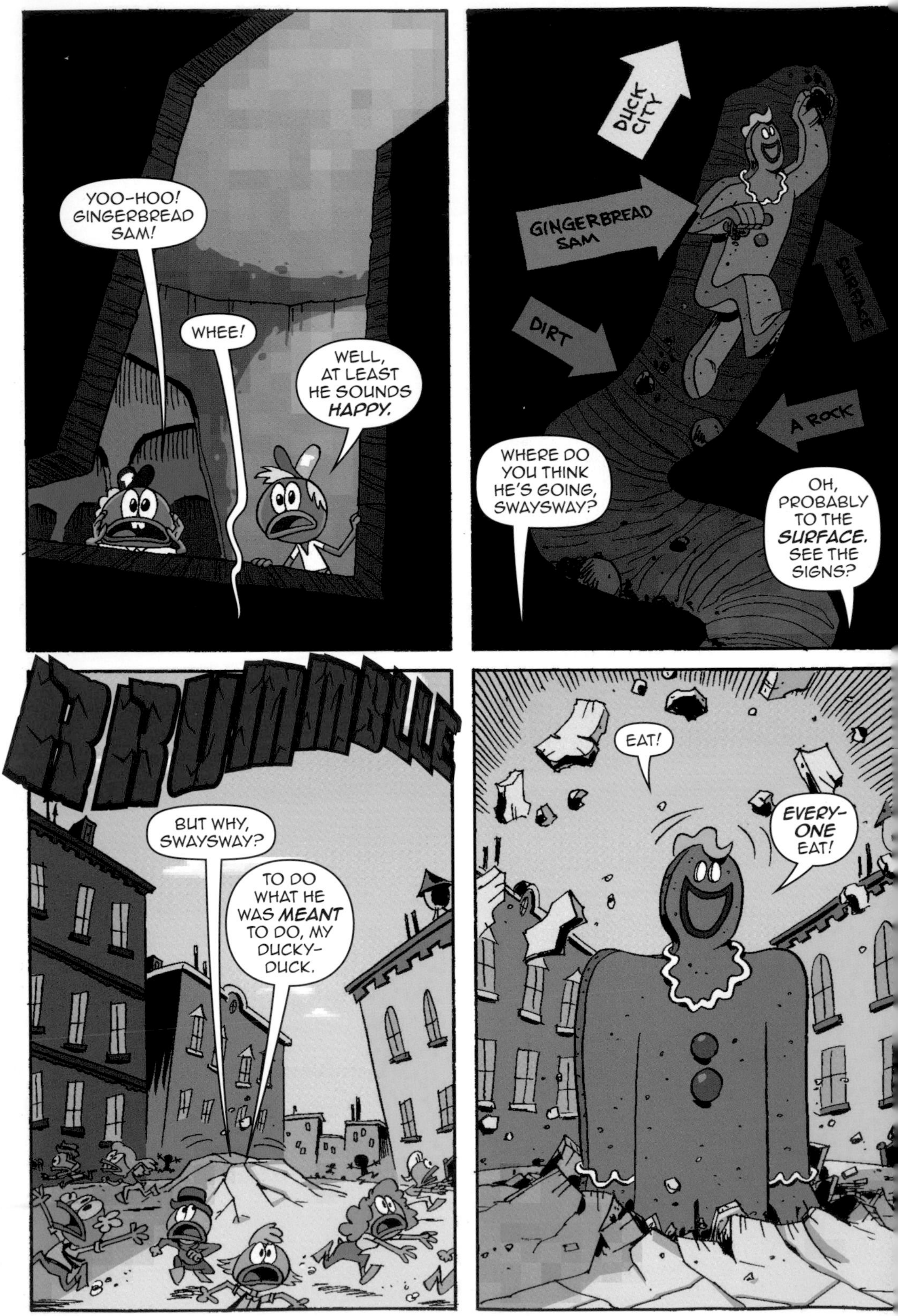
YOO-HOO! GINGERBREAD SAM!
WHEE!
WELL, AT LEAST HE SOUNDS HAPPY.
DUCK CITY
GINGERBREAD SAM
SURFACE
DIRT
A ROCK
WHERE DO YOU THINK HE'S GOING, SWAYSWAY?
OH, PROBABLY TO THE SURFACE. SEE THE SIGNS?
RRUMMBLE
BUT WHY, SWAYSWAY?
TO DO WHAT HE WAS MEANT TO DO, MY DUCKY-DUCK.
EAT!
EVERY-ONE EAT!

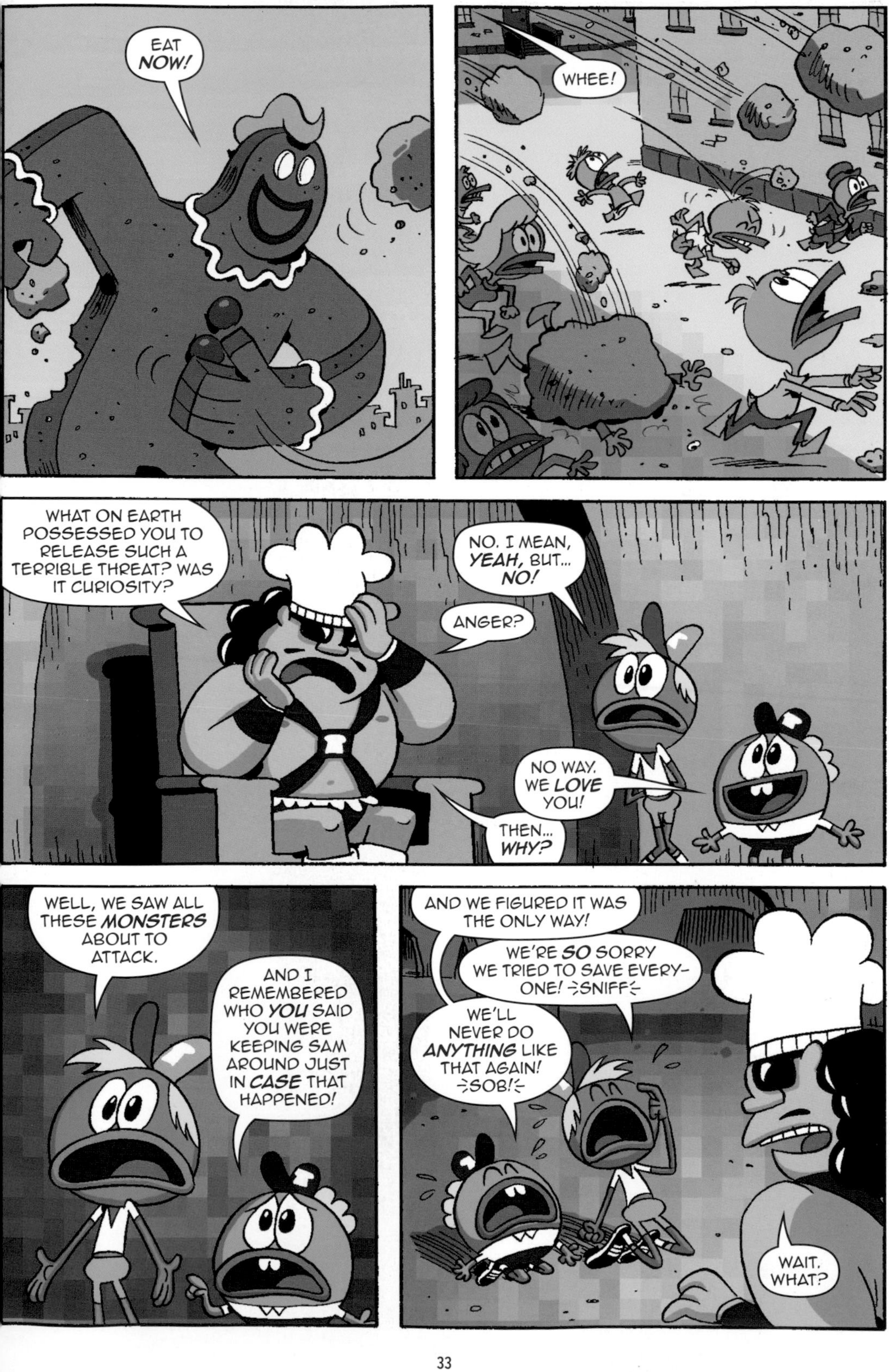
EAT NOW!
WHEE!
WHAT ON EARTH POSSESSED YOU TO RELEASE SUCH A TERRIBLE THREAT? WAS IT CURIOSITY?
NO. I MEAN, YEAH, BUT... NO!
ANGER?
NO WAY. WE LOVE YOU!
THEN... WHY?
WELL, WE SAW ALL THESE MONSTERS ABOUT TO ATTACK.
AND I REMEMBERED WHO YOU SAID YOU WERE KEEPING SAM AROUND JUST IN CASE THAT HAPPENED!
AND WE FIGURED IT WAS THE ONLY WAY!
WE'RE SO SORRY WE TRIED TO SAVE EVERY-ONE! SNIFF
WE'LL NEVER DO ANYTHING LIKE THAT AGAIN! SOB!
WAIT. WHAT?

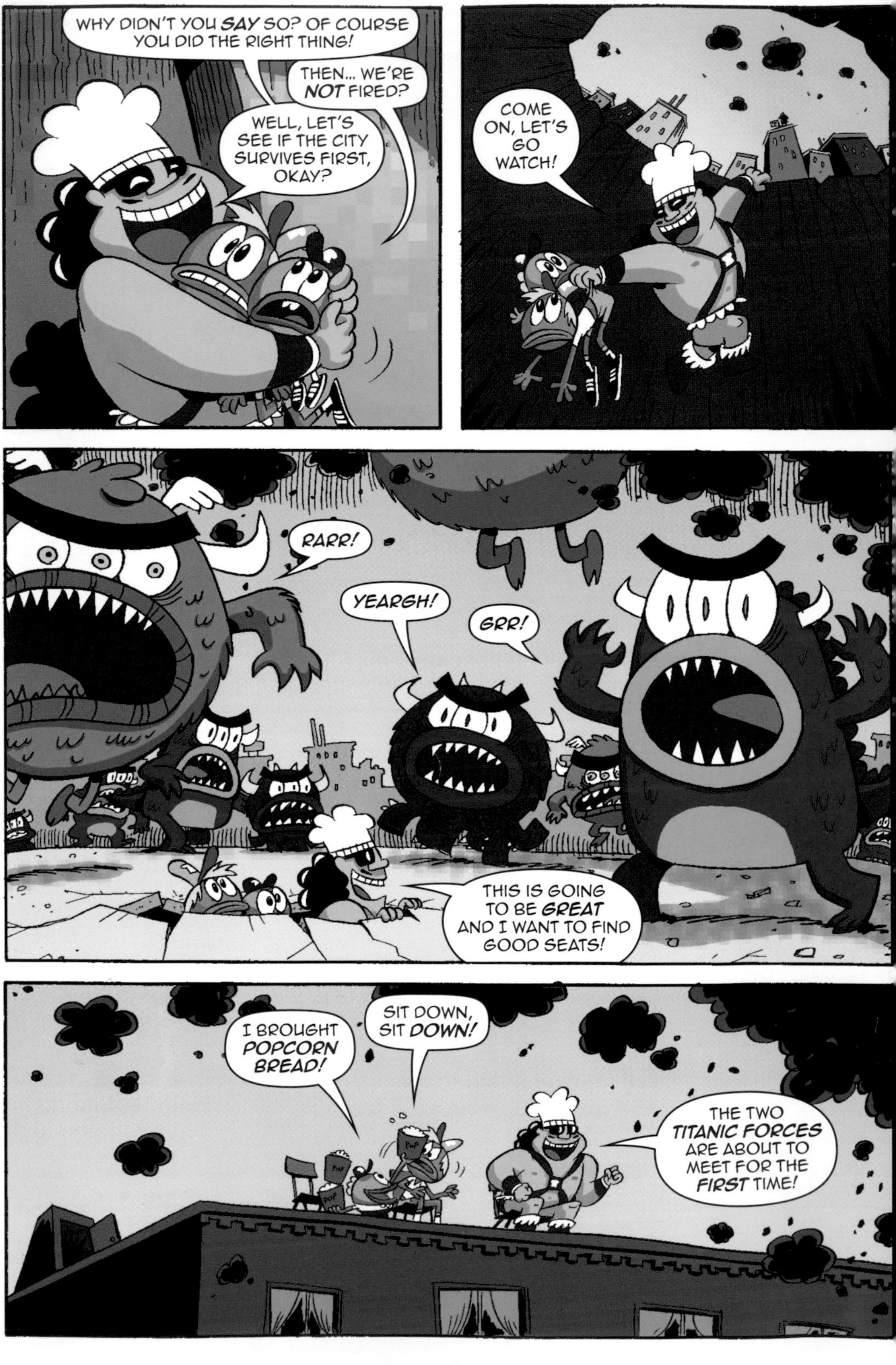
WHY DIDN'T YOU SAY SO? OF COURSE YOU DID THE RIGHT THING!
THEN... WE'RE NOT FIRED?
WELL, LET'S SEE IF THE CITY SURVIVES FIRST, OKAY?
COME ON, LET'S GO WATCH!
RARR!
YEARGH!
GRR!
THIS IS GOING TO BE GREAT AND I WANT TO FIND GOOD SEATS!
I BROUGHT POPCORN BREAD!
SIT DOWN, SIT DOWN!
THE TWO TITANIC FORCES ARE ABOUT TO MEET FOR THE FIRST TIME!

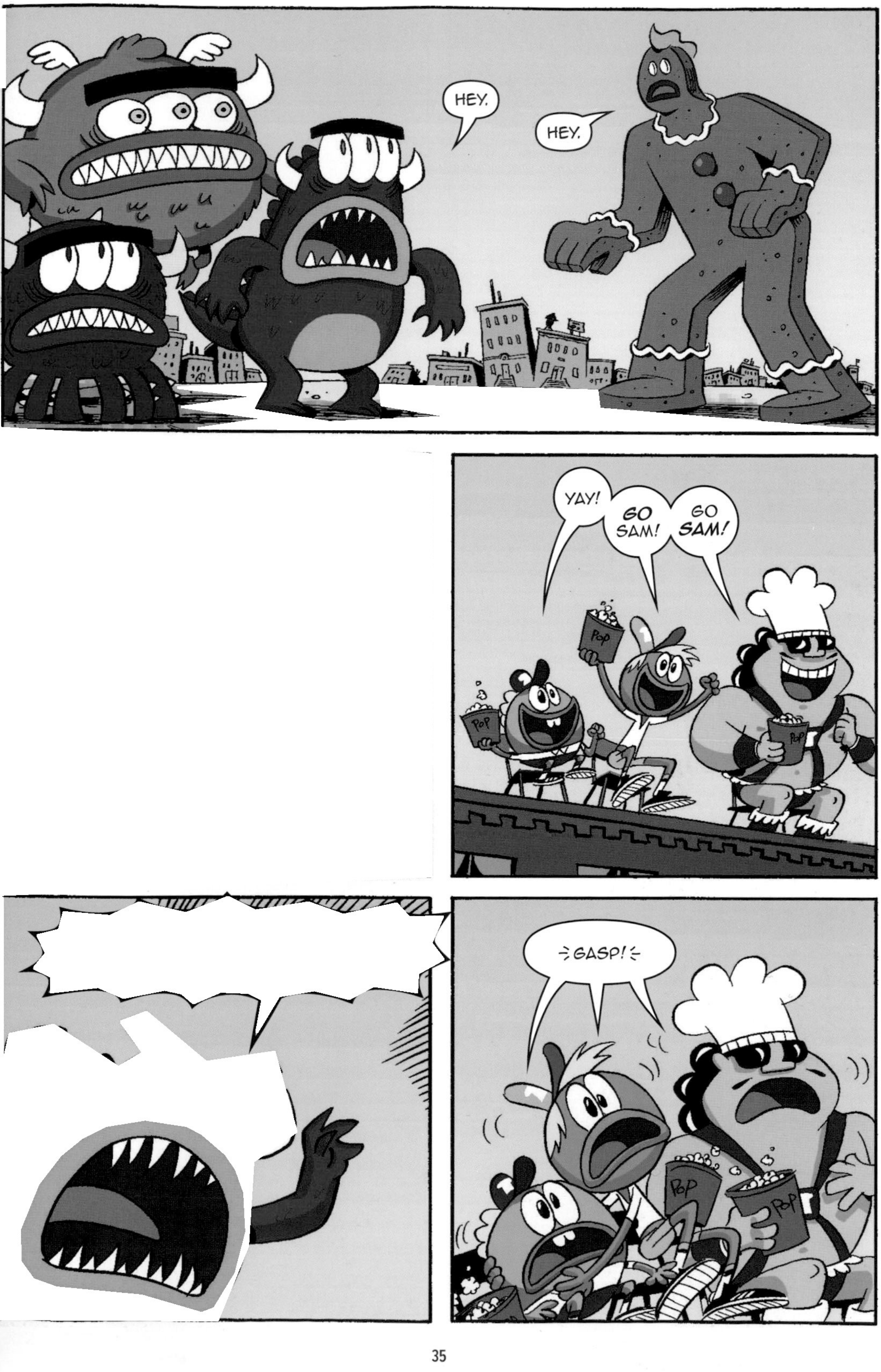
HEY.
HEY.
YAY!
GO SAM!
GO SAM!
GASP!

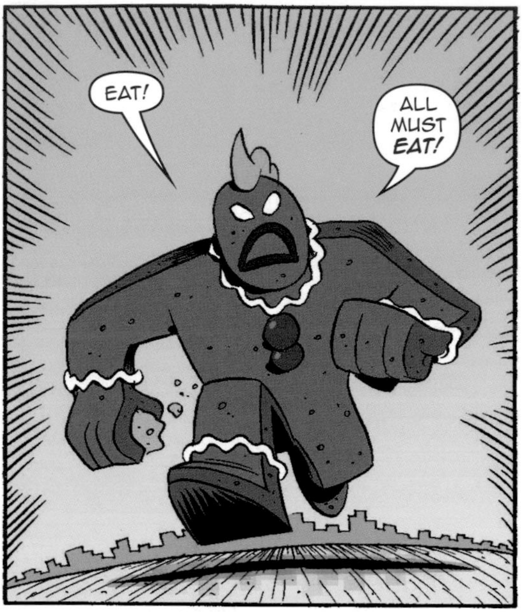
EAT!
ALL MUST EAT!

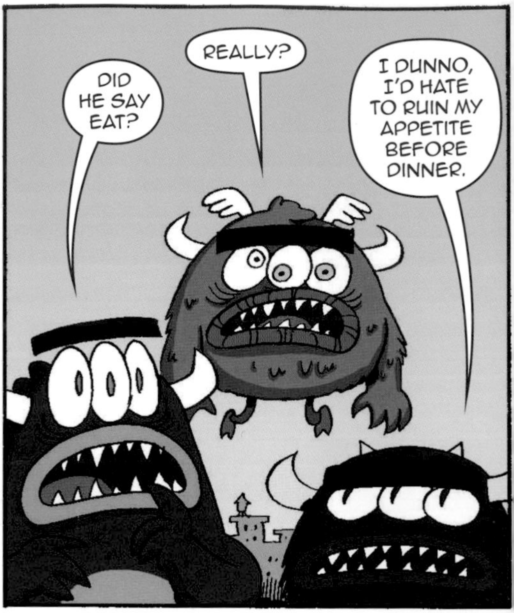
DID HE SAY EAT?
REALLY?
I DUNNO, I'D HATE TO RUIN MY APPETITE BEFORE DINNER.

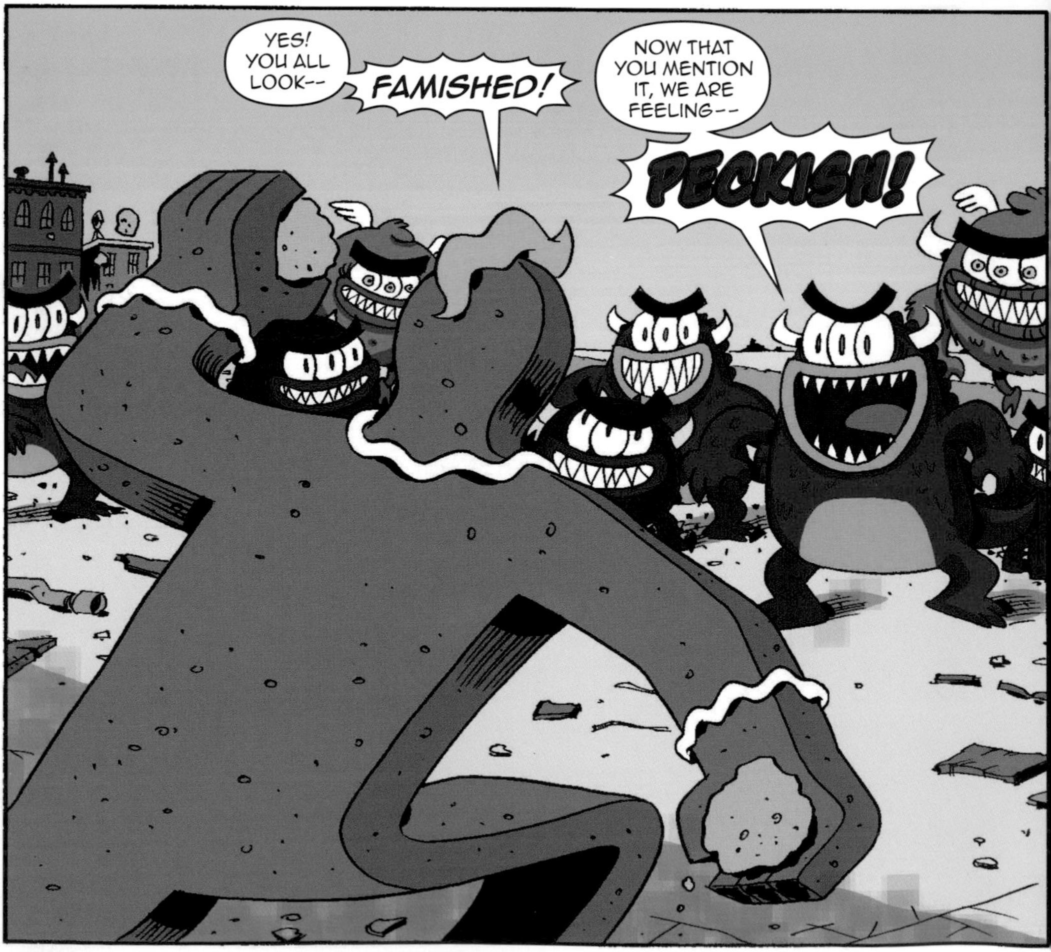
YES! YOU ALL LOOK--
FAMISHED!
NOW THAT YOU MENTION IT, WE ARE FEELING--
PECKISH!

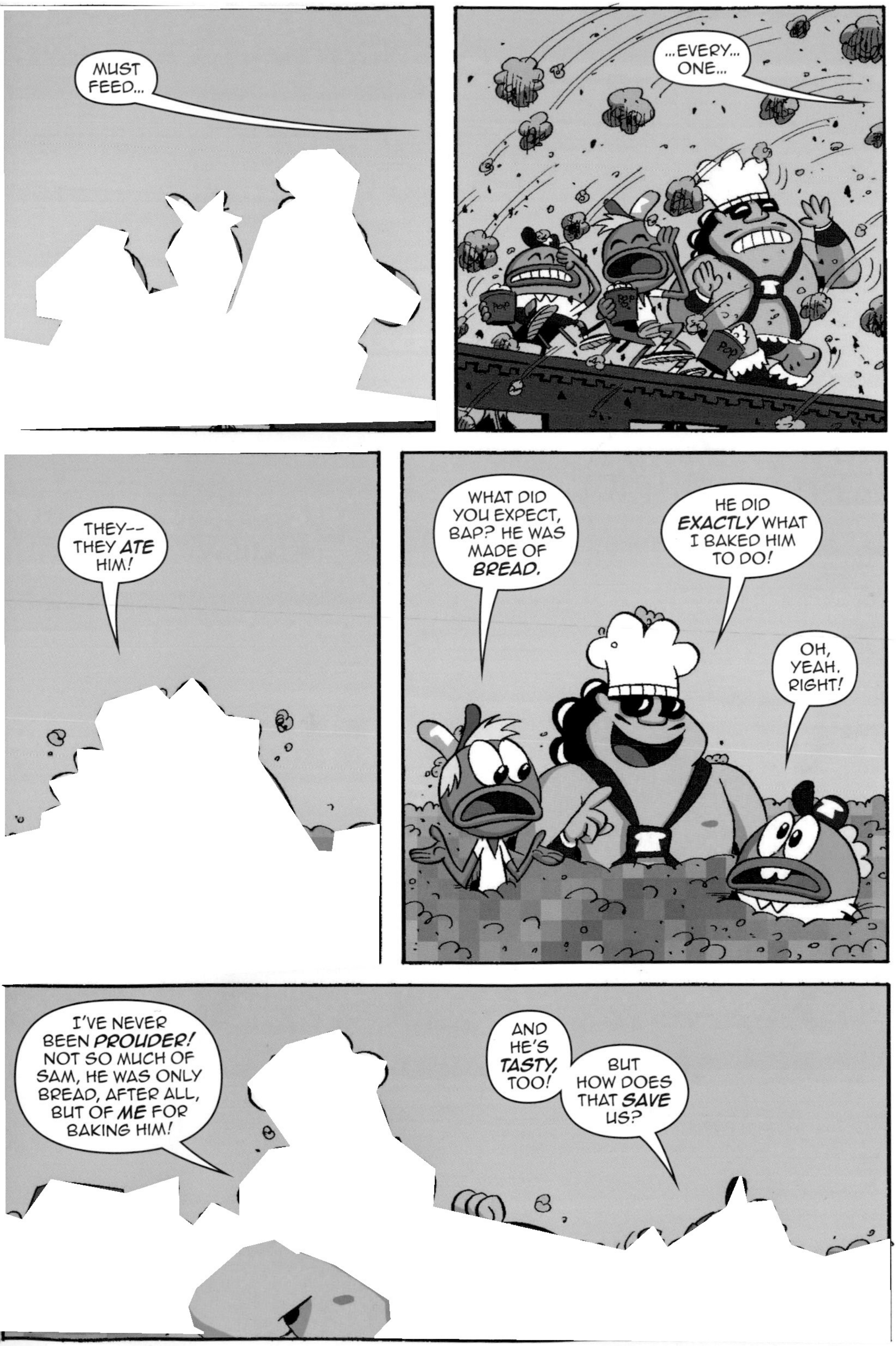
MUST FEED...
...EVERY... ONE...
THEY-- THEY ATE HIM!
WHAT DID YOU EXPECT, BAP? HE WAS MADE OF BREAD.
HE DID EXACTLY WHAT I BAKED HIM TO DO!
OH, YEAH. RIGHT!
I'VE NEVER BEEN PROUDER! NOT SO MUCH OF SAM, HE WAS ONLY BREAD, AFTER ALL, BUT OF ME FOR BAKING HIM!
AND HE'S TASTY, TOO!
BUT HOW DOES THAT SAVE US?

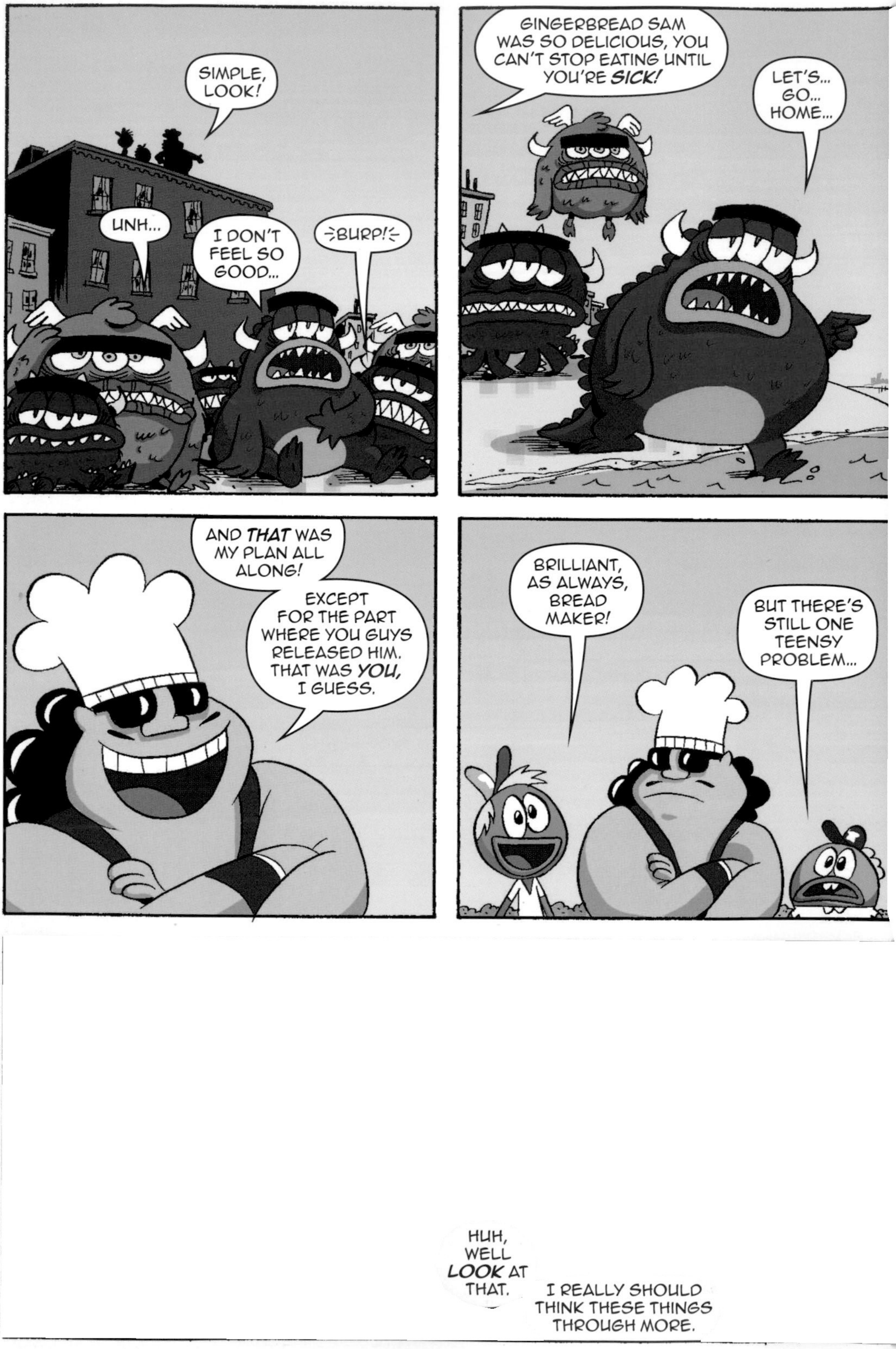
SIMPLE, LOOK!
UNH...
I DON'T FEEL SO GOOD...
BURP!
GINGERBREAD SAM WAS SO DELICIOUS, YOU CAN'T STOP EATING UNTIL YOU'RE SICK!
LET'S... GO... HOME...
AND THAT WAS MY PLAN ALL ALONG!
EXCEPT FOR THE PART WHERE YOU GUYS RELEASED HIM. THAT WAS YOU, I GUESS.
BRILLIANT, AS ALWAYS, BREAD MAKER!
BUT THERE'S STILL ONE TEENSY PROBLEM...
HUH, WELL LOOK AT THAT.
I REALLY SHOULD THINK THESE THINGS THROUGH MORE.

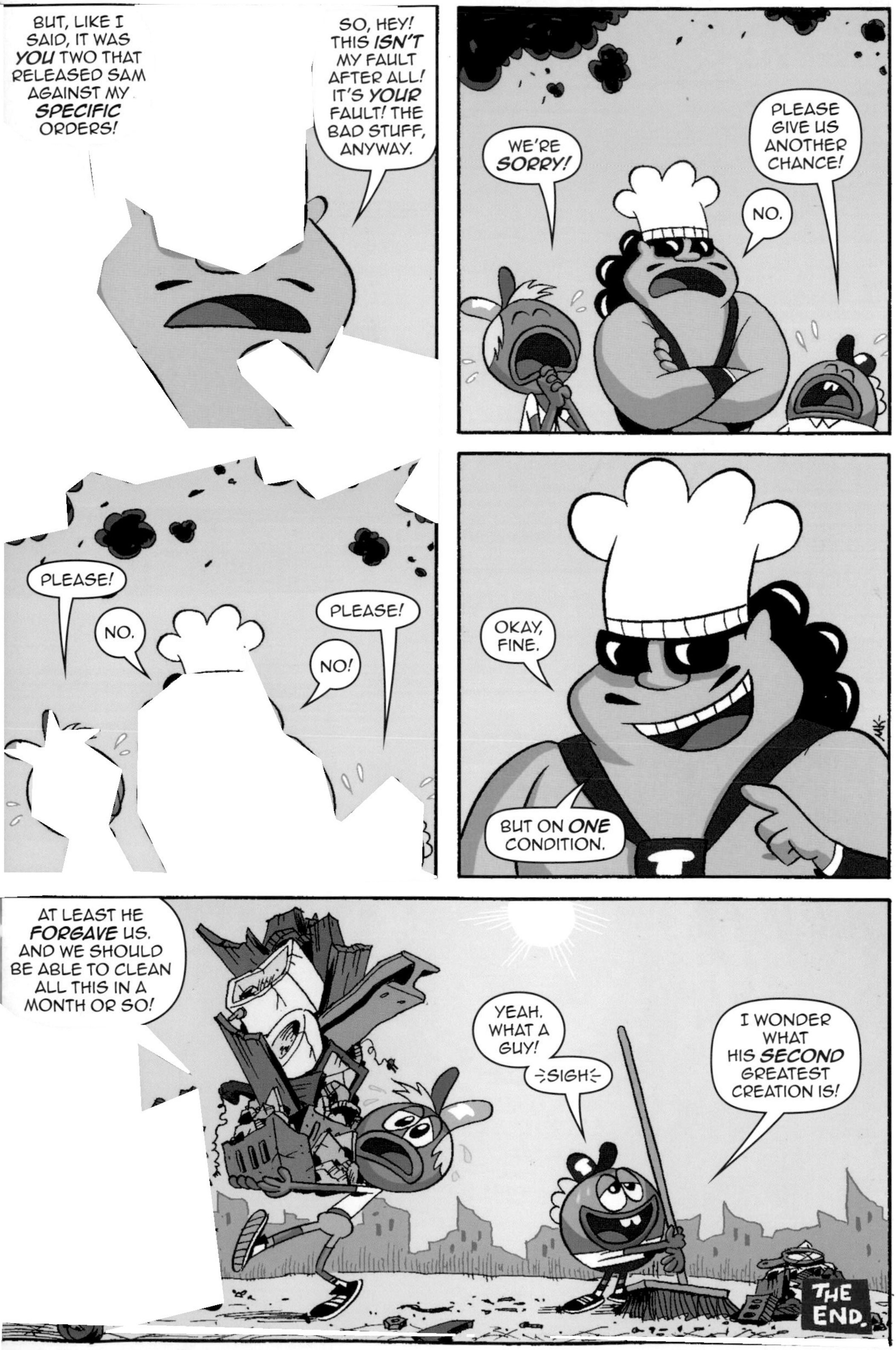
BUT, LIKE I SAID, IT WAS YOU TWO THAT RELEASED SAM AGAINST MY SPECIFIC ORDERS!
SO, HEY! THIS ISN'T MY FAULT AFTER ALL! IT'S YOUR FAULT! THE BAD STUFF, ANYWAY.
WE'RE SORRY!
PLEASE GIVE US ANOTHER CHANCE!
NO.
PLEASE!
NO.
PLEASE!
NO!
OKAY, FINE.
BUT ON ONE CONDITION.
AT LEAST HE FORGAVE US. AND WE SHOULD BE ABLE TO CLEAN ALL THIS IN A MONTH OR SO!
YEAH. WHAT A GUY!
SIGH
I WONDER WHAT HIS SECOND GREATEST CREATION IS!
THE END.

WATCH OUT FOR PAPERCUTZ

Welcome to the slightly-toasted, salt-free second **BREADWINNERS** graphic novel from Papercutz—those somewhat doughy comic-makers dedicated to publishing great graphic novels for all ages. I'm Jim Salicrup, the Silvercup-Bread-loving Editor-in-Chief, and I'm here to share with you all our plans for the future (world domination?) and take you behind the scenes here at Papercutz.

We've got really great news and some somewhat sad news. Just so you don't get anxious, we'll start with the sad news first. This edition of **BREADWINNERS** is the last one Papercutz will be publishing. Hey, don't worry—it's not the end of the world! Especially when you hear our good news...

Coming soon to the bookseller near you will be an all-new Nickelodeon graphic novel series entitled **NICKELODEON PANDEMONIUM!** What's that? You've never heard of that show? That's because it isn't a show, it's an ongoing graphic novel series that will feature comics starring the very best new Nickelodeon cartoon stars—such as Sanjay and Craig, Harvey Peaks, Pig Goat Banana Cricket, and—you guessed it!—Breadwinners!

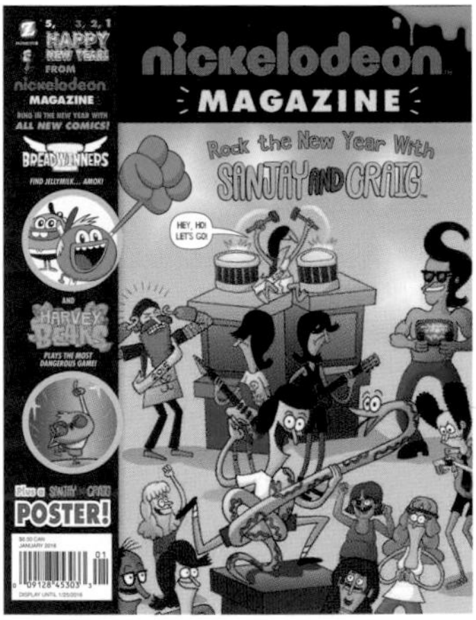

nickelodeon
MAGAZINE
Rock the New Year With
SANJAY AND CRAIG
HEY, HO! LET'S GO!
BREADWINNERS
HARVEY BEAKS
POSTER!

They say variety is the spice of life, so what could be more fun than a graphic novel featuring lots of your favorite Nickelodeon characters? Well, you might argue that the monthly **NICKELODEON MAGAZINE** might be more fun, but the graphic novel will contain **MORE** pages than an issue of the magazine, so you'll be getting **MORE** in the graphic novel series!

Speaking of **NICKELODEON MAGAZINE**, look for Buhdeuce and SwaySway to keep popping up in those pages as well. Let's face it—we love those guys and can't get enough of them. So after you've seen every **BREADWINNERS** cartoon on Nickelodeon, don't forget that Papercutz is **THE** place now to get all-new stories starring your favorite bread-delivering ducks!

Thanks,

Jim

STAY IN TOUCH!

EMAIL:	salicrup@papercutz.com
WEB:	papercutz.com
TWITTER:	@papercutzgn
FACEBOOK:	PAPERCUTZGRAPHICNOVELS
FANMAIL:	Papercutz, 160 Broadway, Suite 700, East Wing, New York, NY 10038

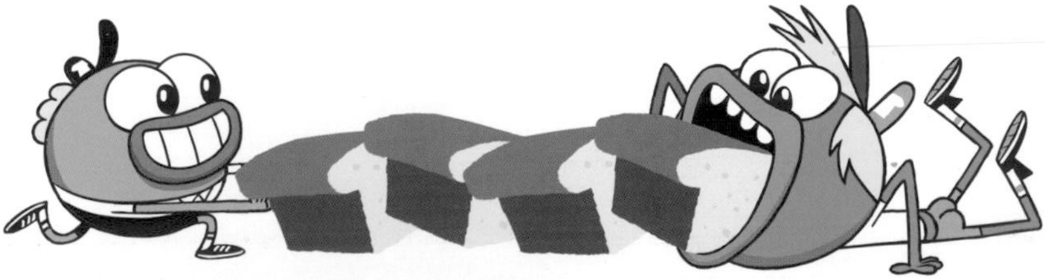

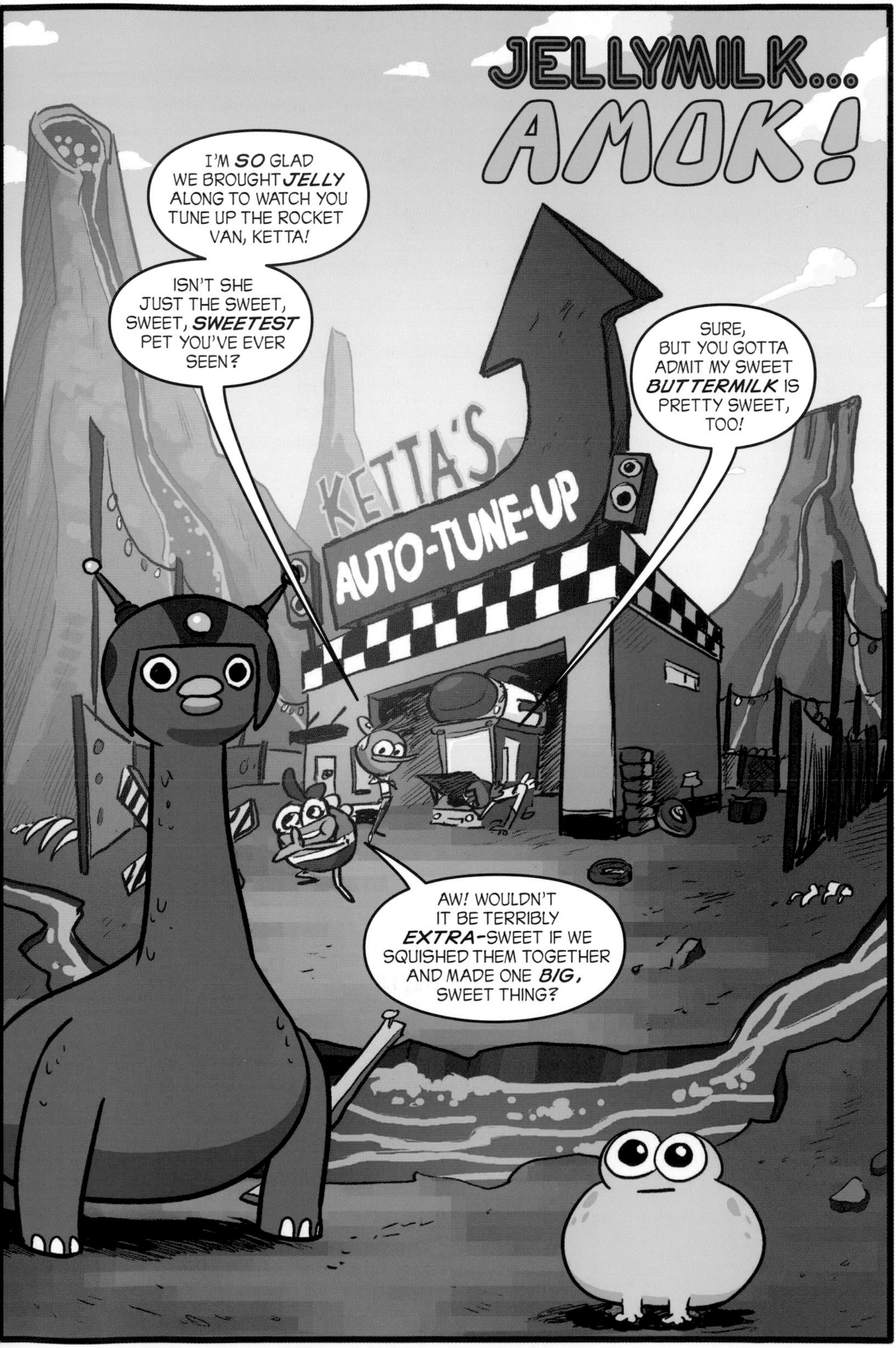
JELLYMILK...
AMOK!
I'M SO GLAD WE BROUGHT JELLY ALONG TO WATCH YOU TUNE UP THE ROCKET VAN, KETTA!
ISN'T SHE JUST THE SWEET, SWEET, SWEETEST PET YOU'VE EVER SEEN?
SURE, BUT YOU GOTTA ADMIT MY SWEET BUTTERMILK IS PRETTY SWEET, TOO!
KETTA'S
AUTO-TUNE-UP
AW! WOULDN'T IT BE TERRIBLY EXTRA-SWEET IF WE SQUISHED THEM TOGETHER AND MADE ONE BIG, SWEET THING?

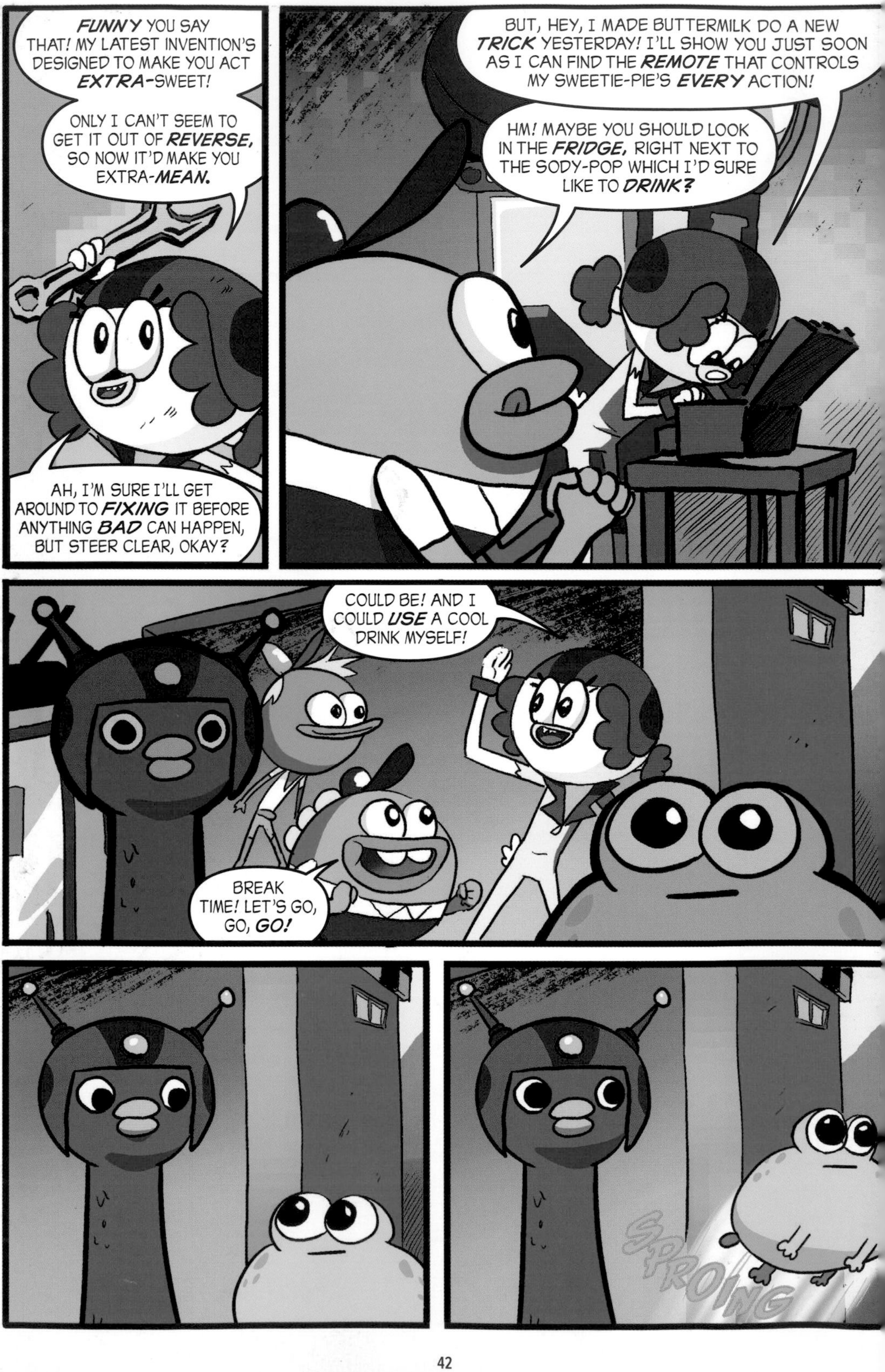
FUNNY YOU SAY THAT! MY LATEST INVENTION'S DESIGNED TO MAKE YOU ACT EXTRA-SWEET!
ONLY I CAN'T SEEM TO GET IT OUT OF REVERSE, SO NOW IT'D MAKE YOU EXTRA-MEAN.
AH, I'M SURE I'LL GET AROUND TO FIXING IT BEFORE ANYTHING BAD CAN HAPPEN, BUT STEER CLEAR, OKAY?
BUT, HEY, I MADE BUTTERMILK DO A NEW TRICK YESTERDAY! I'LL SHOW YOU JUST SOON AS I CAN FIND THE REMOTE THAT CONTROLS MY SWEETIE-PIE'S EVERY ACTION!
HM! MAYBE YOU SHOULD LOOK IN THE FRIDGE, RIGHT NEXT TO THE SODY-POP WHICH I'D SURE LIKE TO DRINK?
COULD BE! AND I COULD USE A COOL DRINK MYSELF!
BREAK TIME! LET'S GO, GO, GO!
SPROING

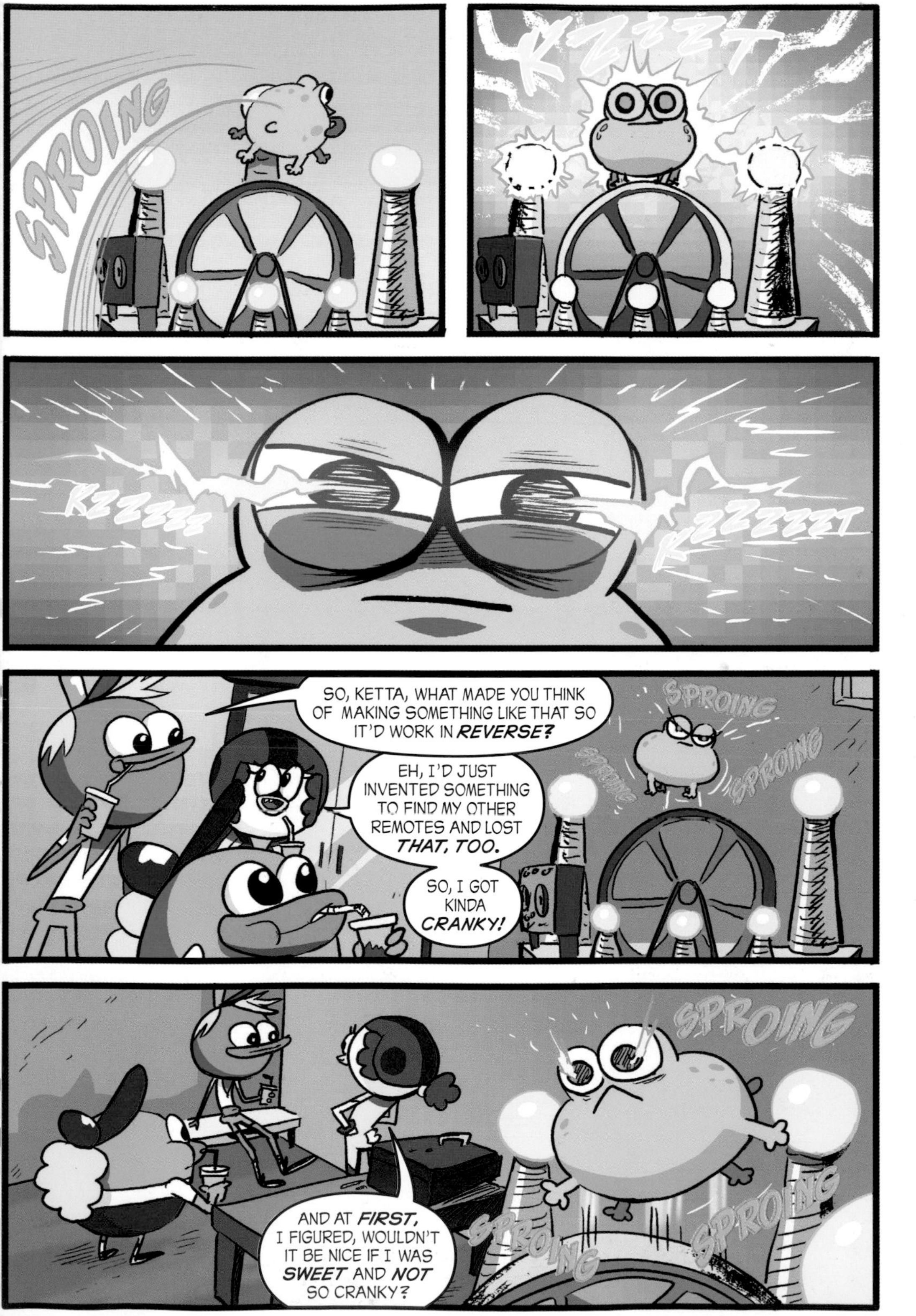
SPROING
KZZZZT
KZZZZZZ
KZZZZZZT
SO, KETTA, WHAT MADE YOU THINK OF MAKING SOMETHING LIKE THAT SO IT'D WORK IN *REVERSE?*
SPROING
SPROING
SPROING
EH, I'D JUST INVENTED SOMETHING TO FIND MY OTHER REMOTES AND LOST *THAT, TOO.*
SO, I GOT KINDA *CRANKY!*
SPROING
AND AT *FIRST,* I FIGURED, WOULDN'T IT BE NICE IF I WAS *SWEET* AND *NOT* SO CRANKY?
SPROING
SPROING

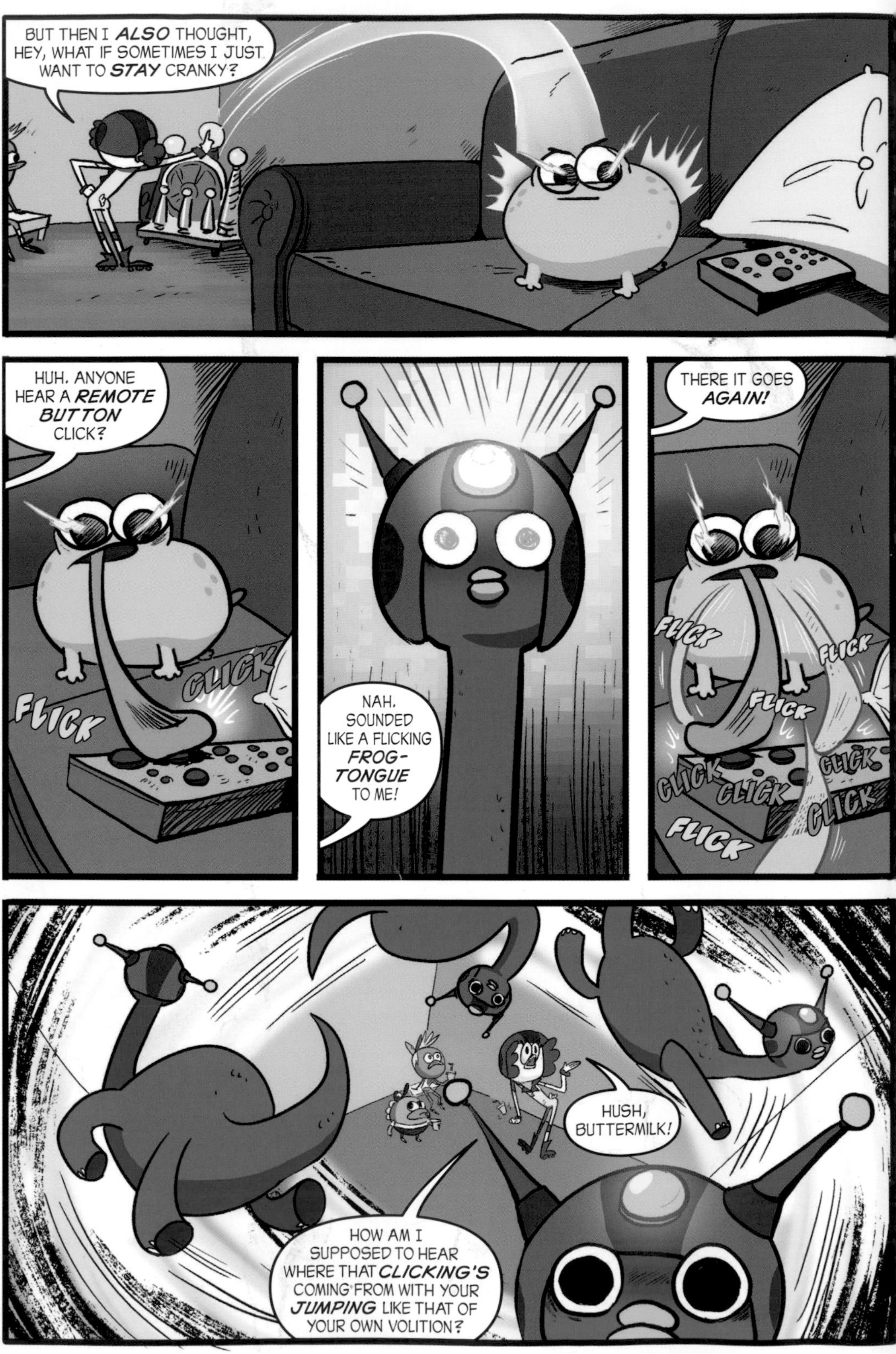
BUT THEN I ALSO THOUGHT, HEY, WHAT IF SOMETIMES I JUST WANT TO STAY CRANKY?
HUH. ANYONE HEAR A REMOTE BUTTON CLICK?
CLICK
FLICK
NAH. SOUNDED LIKE A FLICKING FROG-TONGUE TO ME!
THERE IT GOES AGAIN!
FLICK
FLICK
FLICK
CLICK
CLICK
CLICK
CLICK
FLICK
HUSH, BUTTERMILK!
HOW AM I SUPPOSED TO HEAR WHERE THAT CLICKING'S COMING FROM WITH YOUR JUMPING LIKE THAT OF YOUR OWN VOLITION?

HEY, *JELLY* FOUND YOUR REMOTE!

I *TOLD* YOU SHE'S THE SWEETEST!

I BET SHE'S GOING TO *RETURN* IT TO YOU RIGHT NOW!

AW!

SILLY *JELLY!*

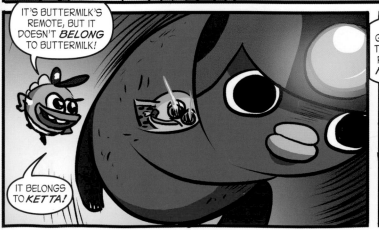

IT'S BUTTERMILK'S REMOTE, BUT IT DOESN'T *BELONG* TO BUTTERMILK!

IT BELONGS TO *KETTA!*

SO GIVE IT TO HER RIGHT *NOW!*

FLICK CLICK

HUH. THERE'RE THOSE *SOUNDS* AGAIN!

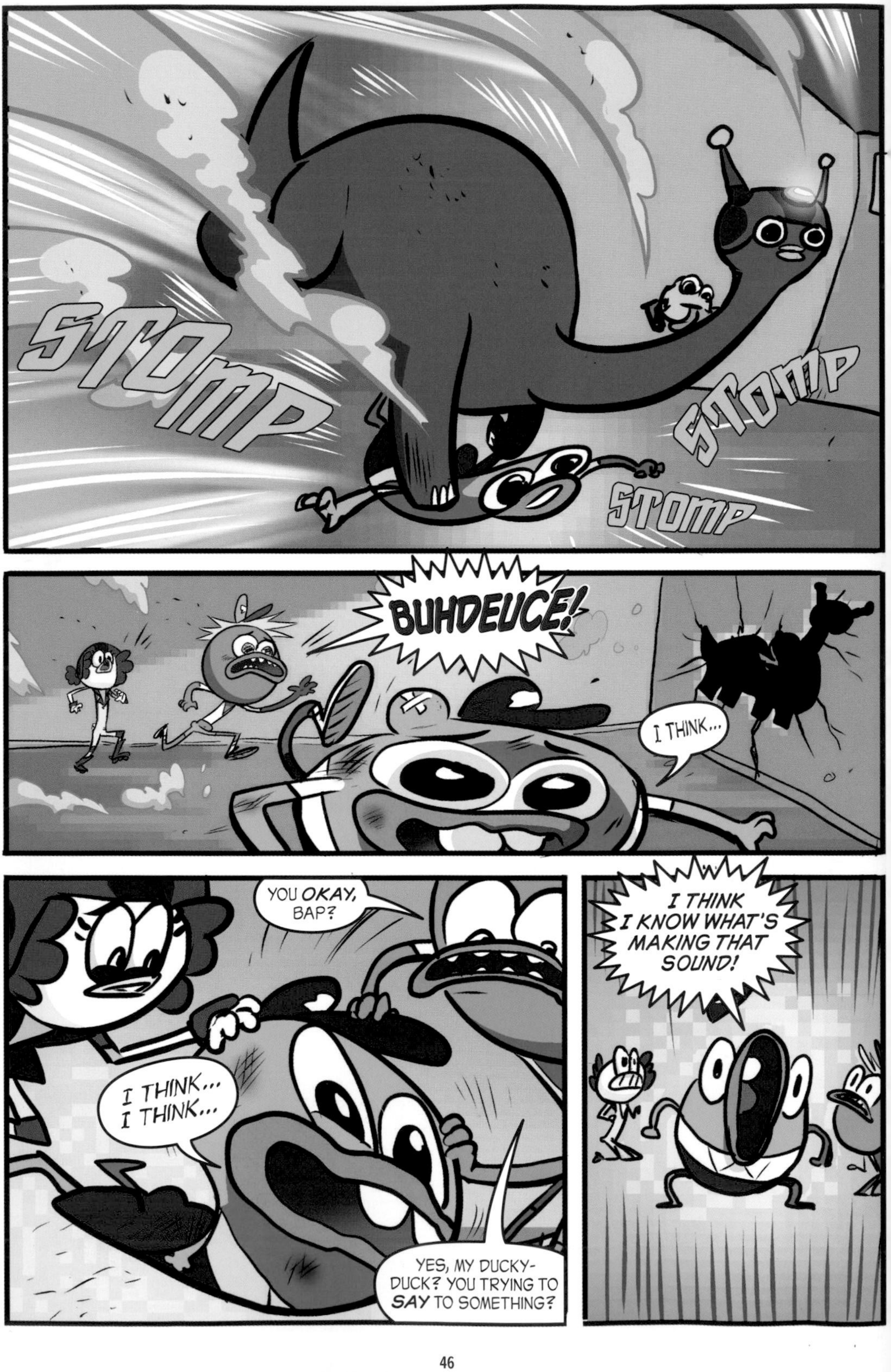
STOMP
STOMP
STOMP
BUHDEUCE!
I THINK...
YOU OKAY, BAP?
I THINK... I THINK...
YES, MY DUCKY-DUCK? YOU TRYING TO SAY TO SOMETHING?
I THINK I KNOW WHAT'S MAKING THAT SOUND!

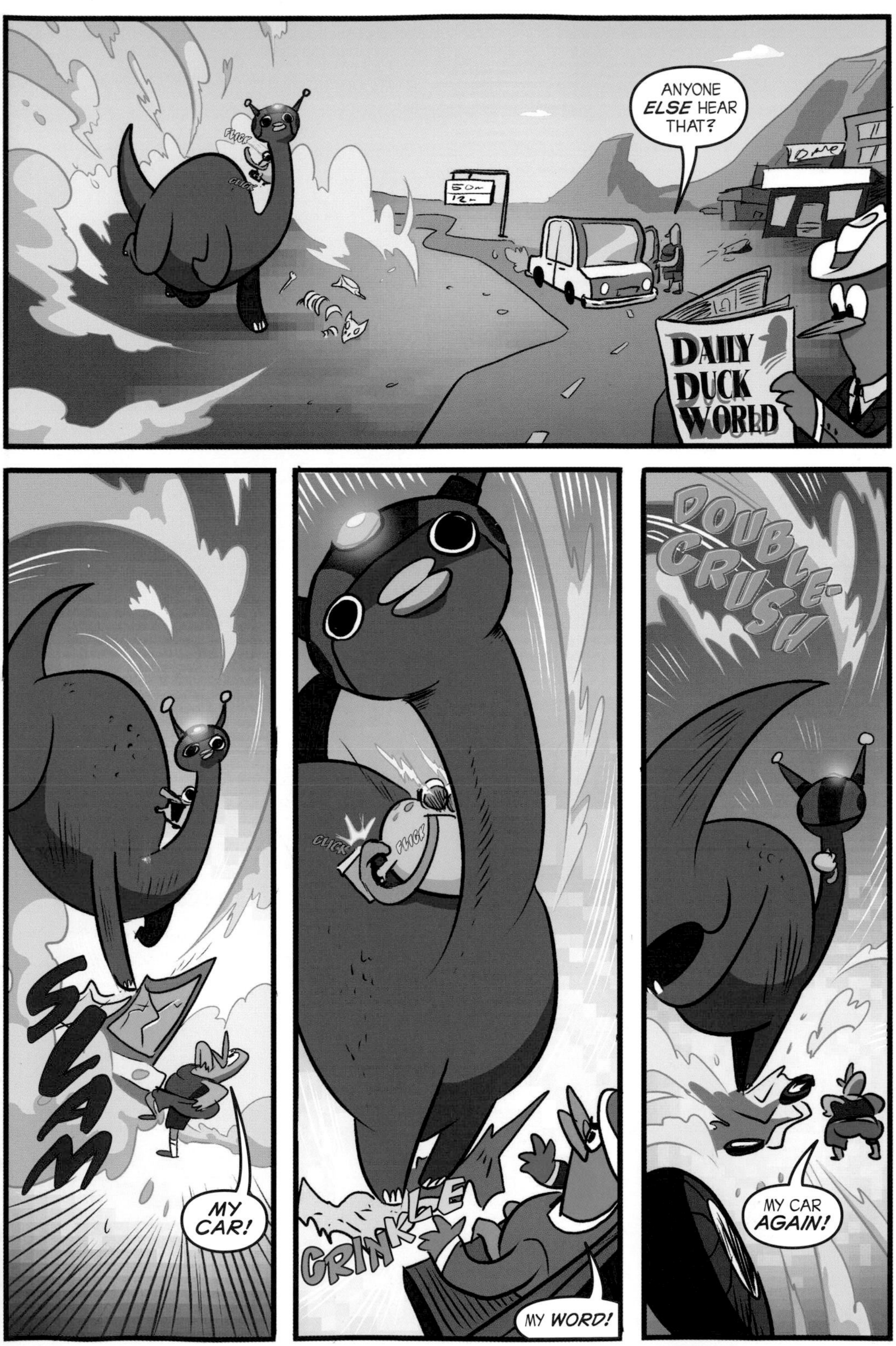
ANYONE ELSE HEAR THAT?
DAILY DUCK WORLD
FLICK
CLICK
SLAM
MY CAR!
CLICK
FLICK
CRINKLE
MY WORD!
DOUBLE-CRUSH
MY CAR AGAIN!

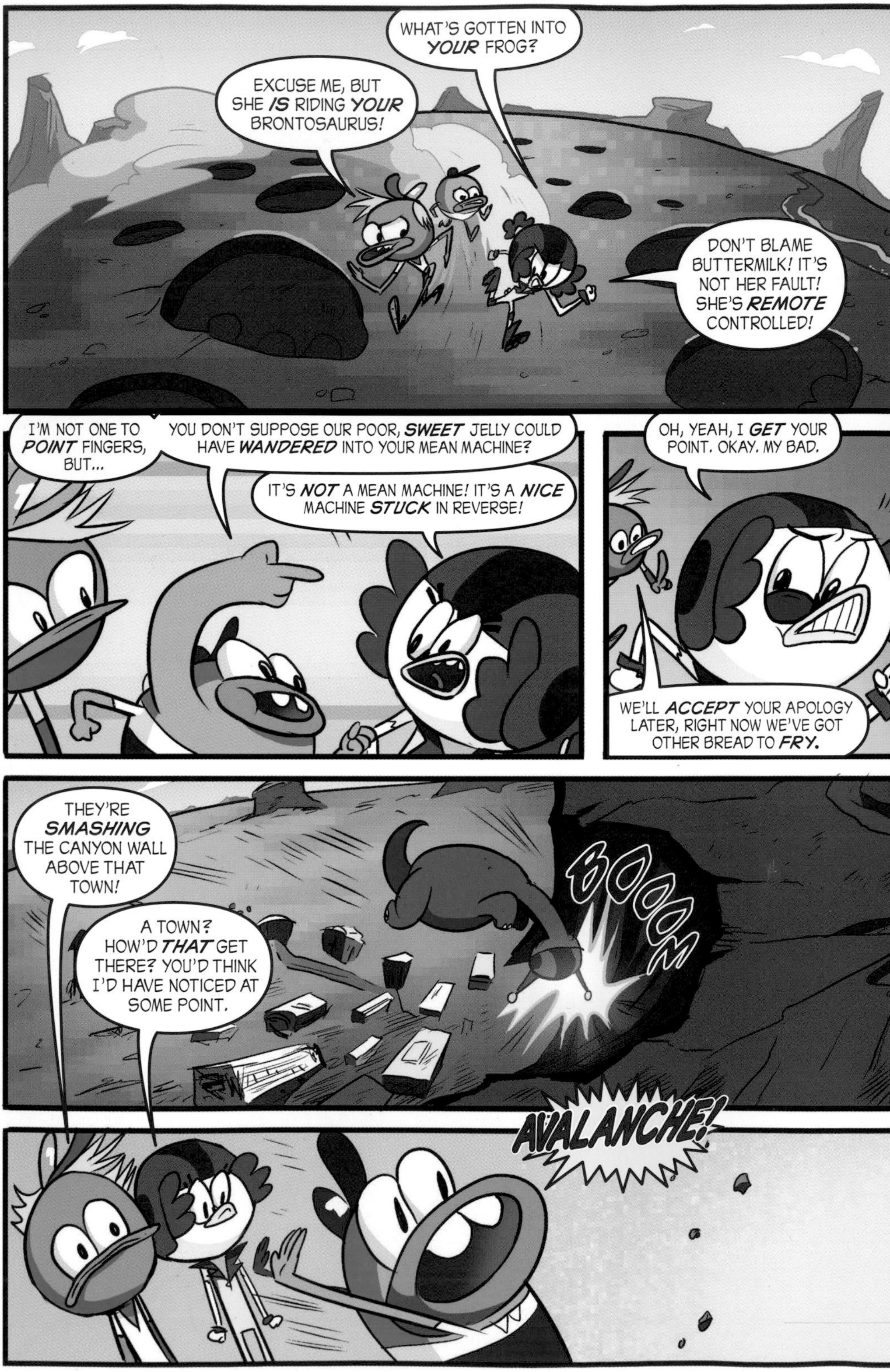
WHAT'S GOTTEN INTO YOUR FROG?
EXCUSE ME, BUT SHE IS RIDING YOUR BRONTOSAURUS!
DON'T BLAME BUTTERMILK! IT'S NOT HER FAULT! SHE'S REMOTE CONTROLLED!
I'M NOT ONE TO POINT FINGERS, BUT...
YOU DON'T SUPPOSE OUR POOR, SWEET JELLY COULD HAVE WANDERED INTO YOUR MEAN MACHINE?
IT'S NOT A MEAN MACHINE! IT'S A NICE MACHINE STUCK IN REVERSE!
OH, YEAH, I GET YOUR POINT. OKAY. MY BAD.
WE'LL ACCEPT YOUR APOLOGY LATER, RIGHT NOW WE'VE GOT OTHER BREAD TO FRY.
THEY'RE SMASHING THE CANYON WALL ABOVE THAT TOWN!
A TOWN? HOW'D THAT GET THERE? YOU'D THINK I'D HAVE NOTICED AT SOME POINT.
BOOOM
AVALANCHE!

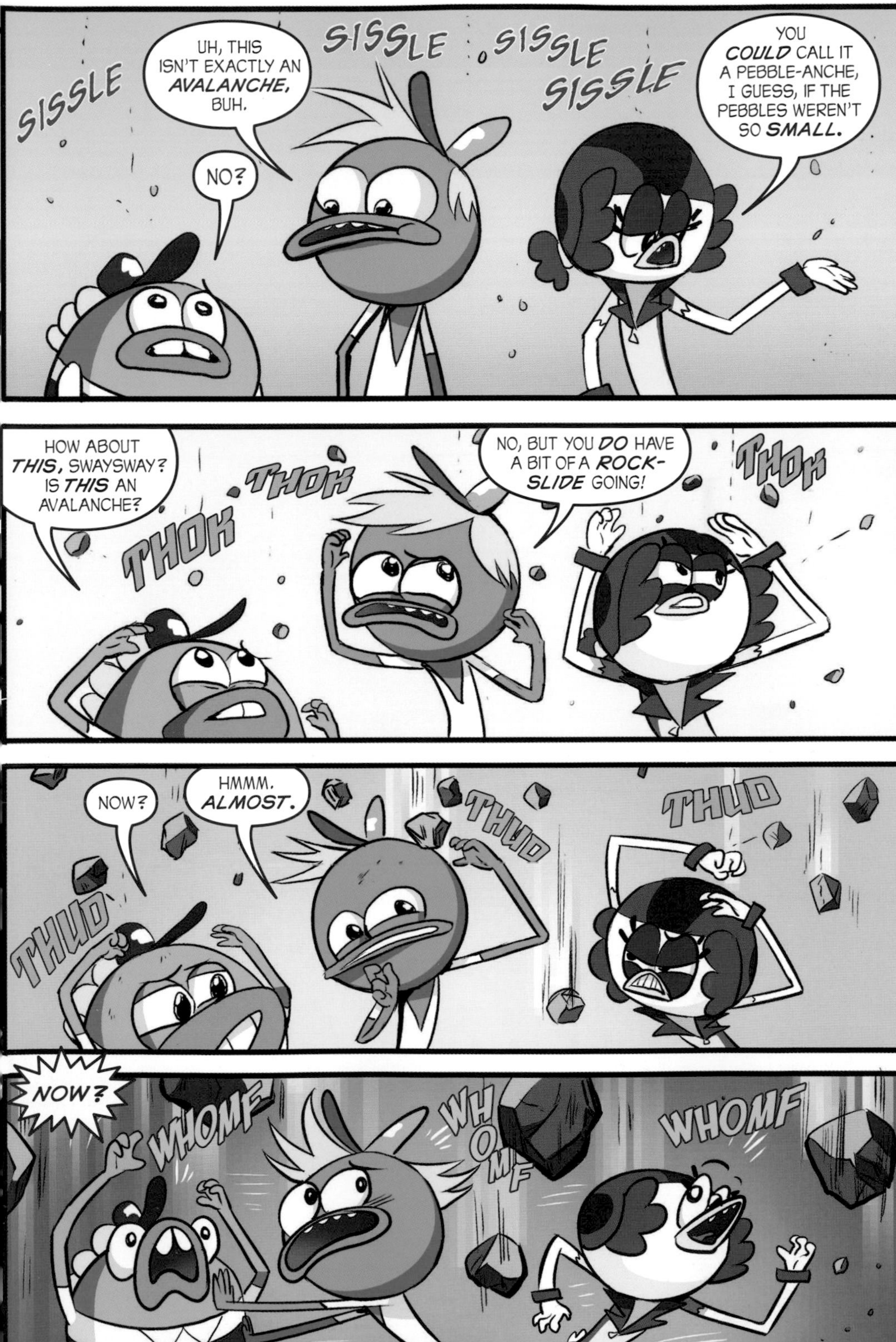
SISSLE
UH, THIS ISN'T EXACTLY AN AVALANCHE, BUH.
SISSLE SISSLE
SISSLE
NO?
YOU COULD CALL IT A PEBBLE-ANCHE, I GUESS, IF THE PEBBLES WEREN'T SO SMALL.
HOW ABOUT THIS, SWAYSWAY? IS THIS AN AVALANCHE?
THOK
THOK
NO, BUT YOU DO HAVE A BIT OF A ROCK-SLIDE GOING!
THOK
NOW?
HMMM. ALMOST.
THUD
THUD
THUD
NOW?
WHOMF
WHOMF
WHOMF

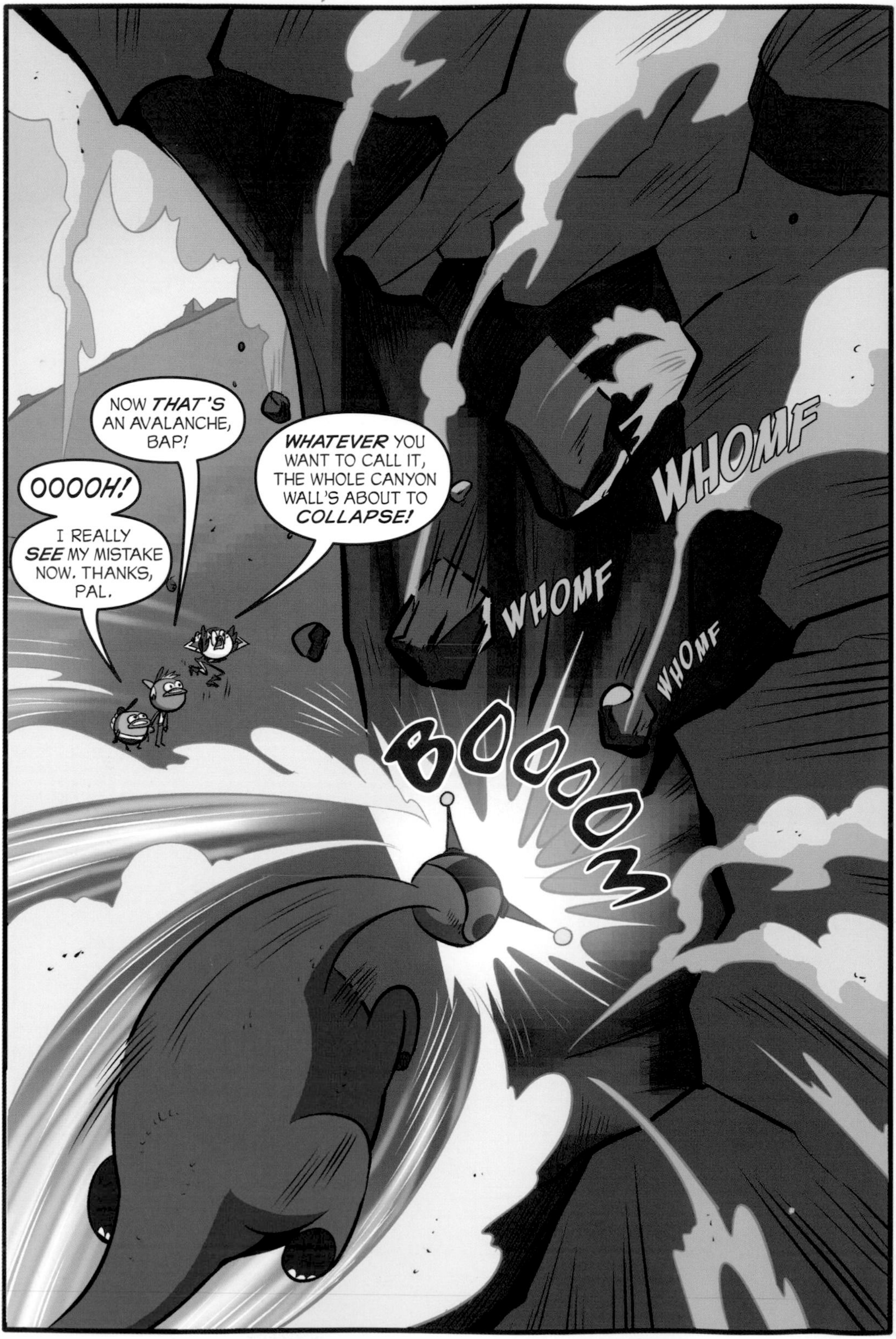

NOW *THAT'S* AN AVALANCHE, BAP!
OOOOH!
I REALLY *SEE* MY MISTAKE NOW. THANKS, PAL.
WHATEVER YOU WANT TO CALL IT, THE WHOLE CANYON WALL'S ABOUT TO *COLLAPSE!*
WHOMF
WHOMF
WHOMF
BOOOOM

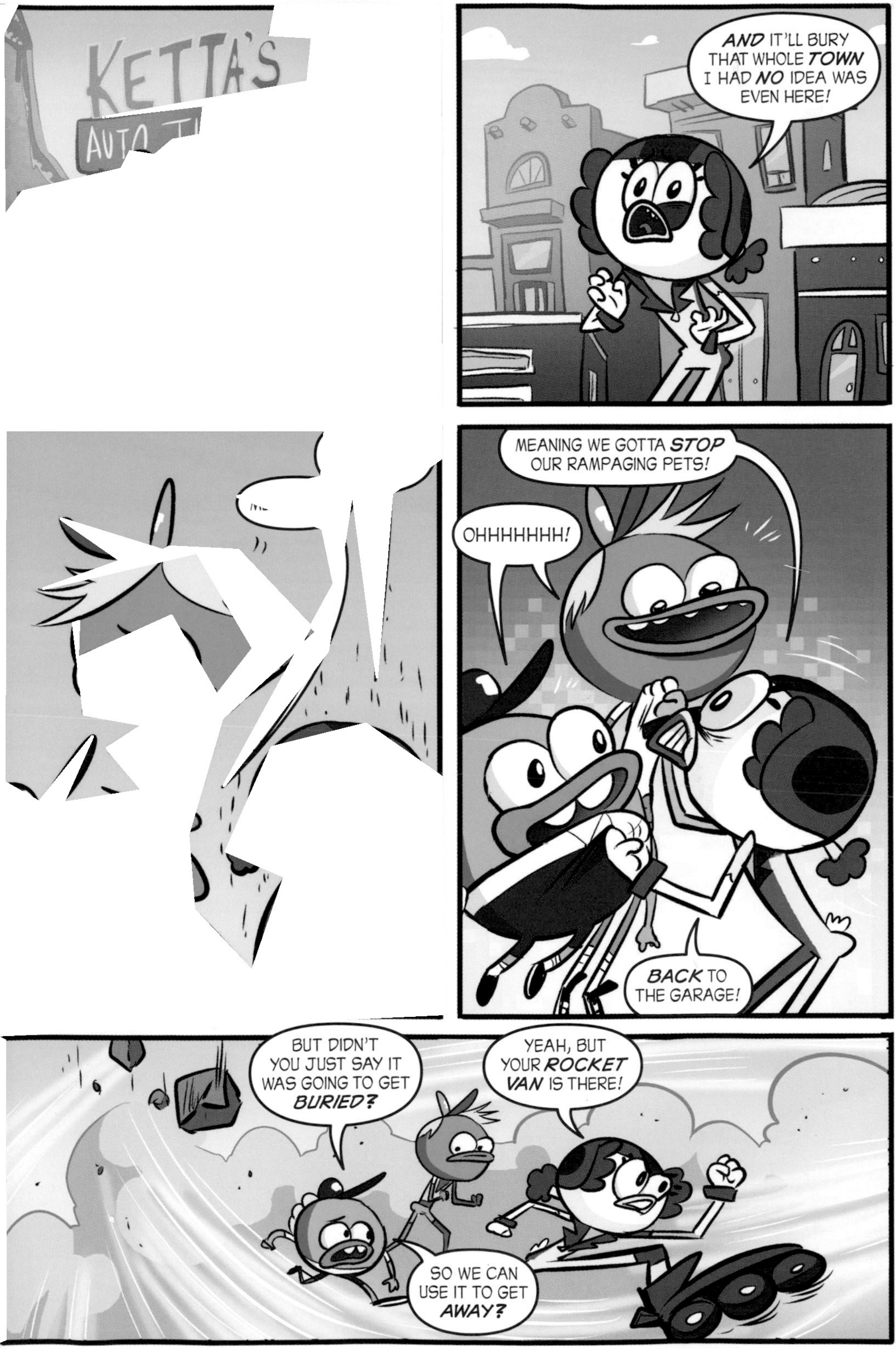
KETTA'S
AND IT'LL BURY THAT WHOLE TOWN I HAD NO IDEA WAS EVEN HERE!
MEANING WE GOTTA STOP OUR RAMPAGING PETS!
OHHHHHHH!
BACK TO THE GARAGE!
BUT DIDN'T YOU JUST SAY IT WAS GOING TO GET BURIED?
YEAH, BUT YOUR ROCKET VAN IS THERE!
SO WE CAN USE IT TO GET AWAY?

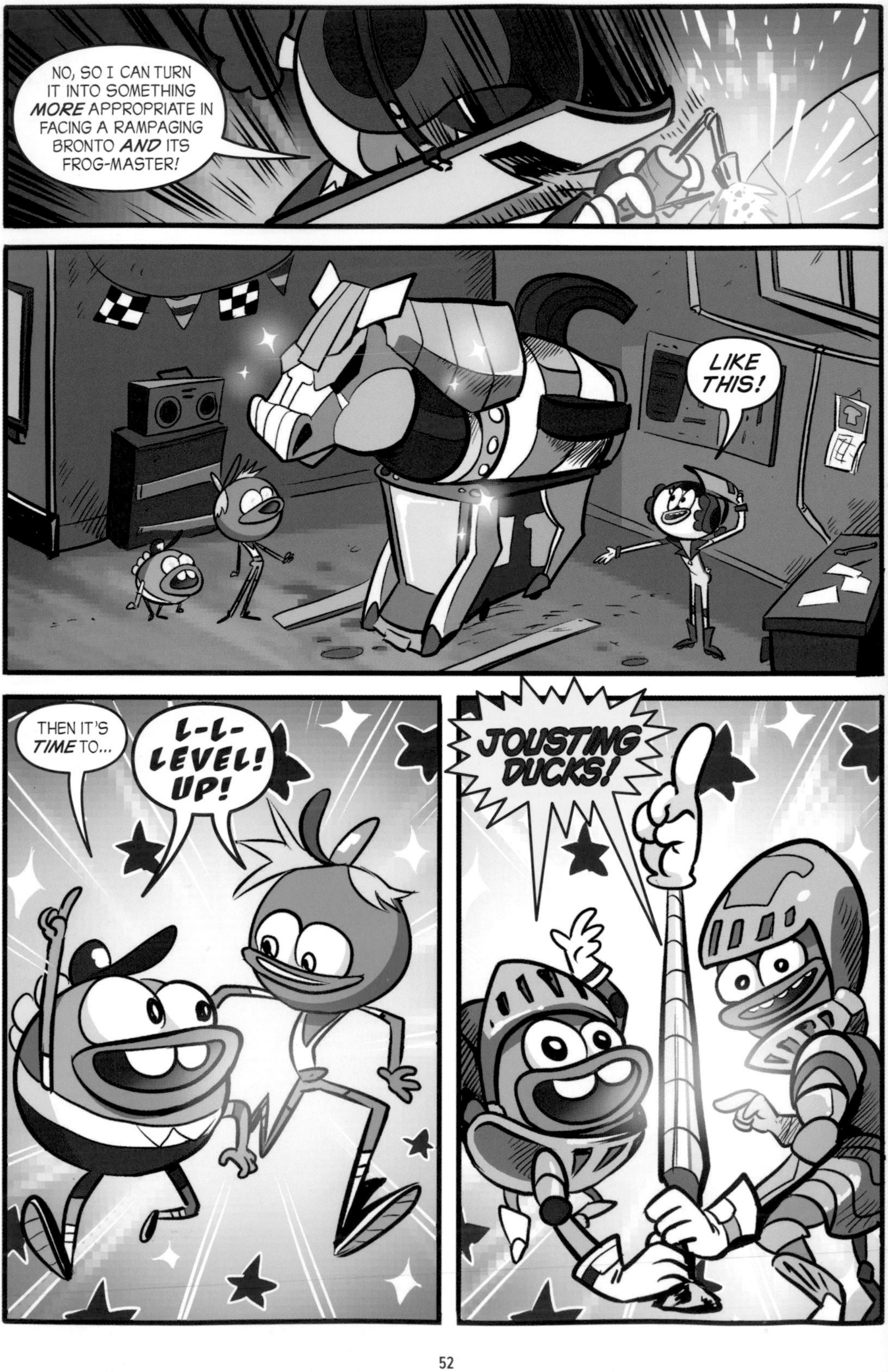
NO, SO I CAN TURN IT INTO SOMETHING *MORE* APPROPRIATE IN FACING A RAMPAGING BRONTO *AND* ITS FROG-MASTER!
LIKE THIS!
THEN IT'S *TIME* TO...
L-L-LEVEL! UP!
JOUSTING DUCKS!

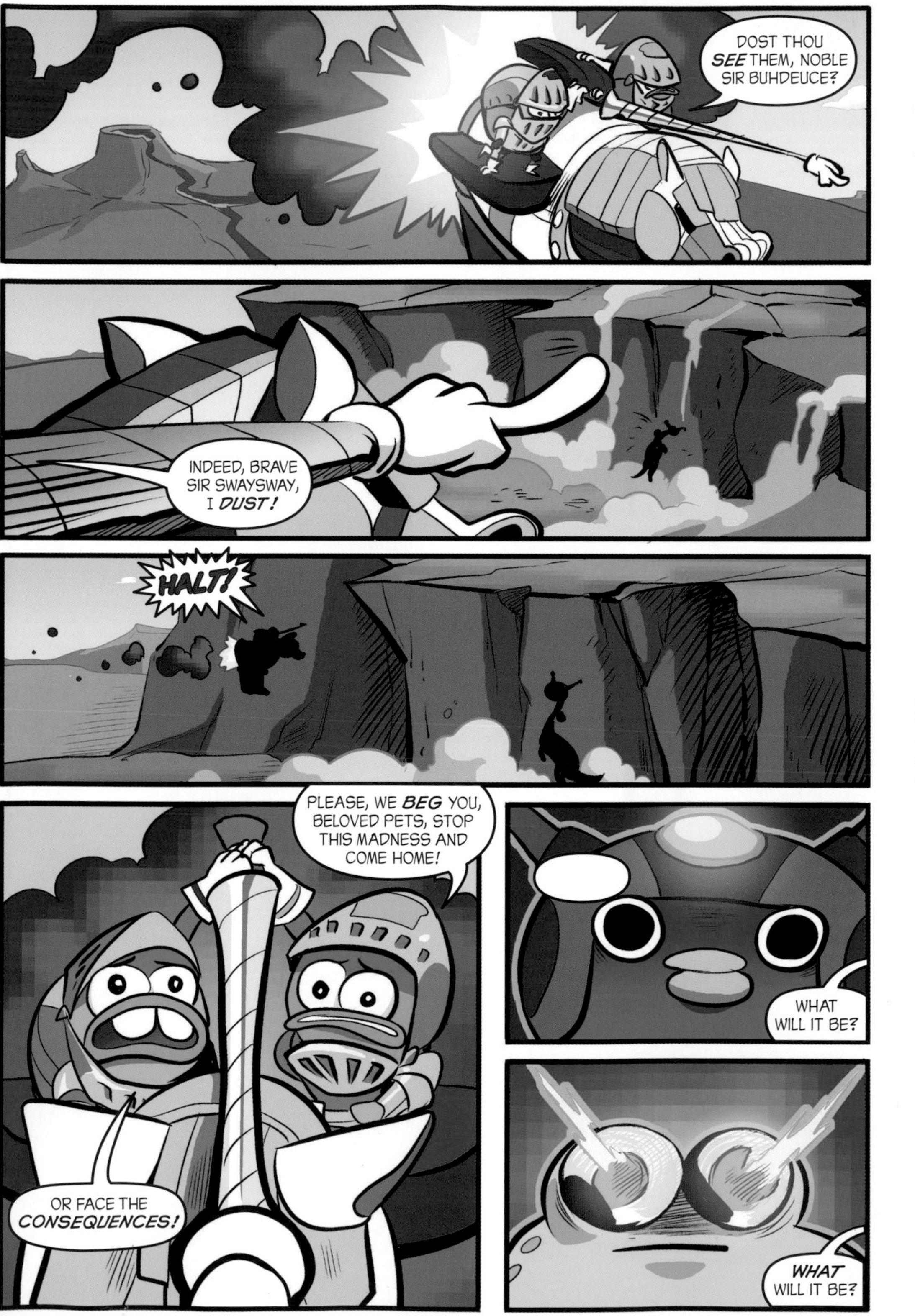
DOST THOU SEE THEM, NOBLE SIR BUHDEUCE?
INDEED, BRAVE SIR SWAYSWAY, I DUST!
HALT!
PLEASE, WE BEG YOU, BELOVED PETS, STOP THIS MADNESS AND COME HOME!
OR FACE THE CONSEQUENCES!
WHAT WILL IT BE?
WHAT WILL IT BE?

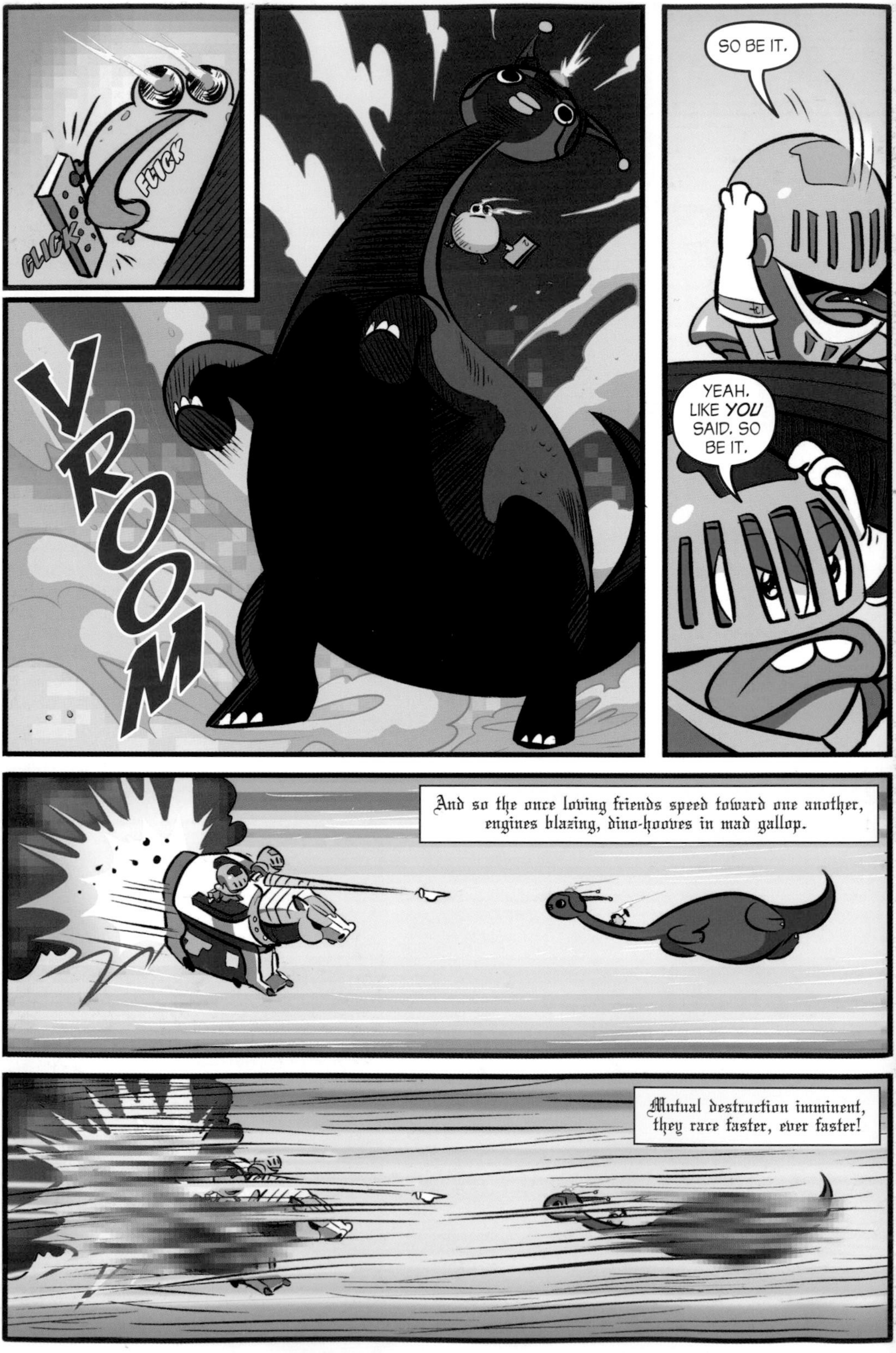
CLICK
FLICK
VROOM
SO BE IT.
YEAH. LIKE *YOU* SAID. SO BE IT.
And so the once loving friends speed toward one another, engines blazing, dino-hooves in mad gallop.
Mutual destruction imminent, they race faster, ever faster!

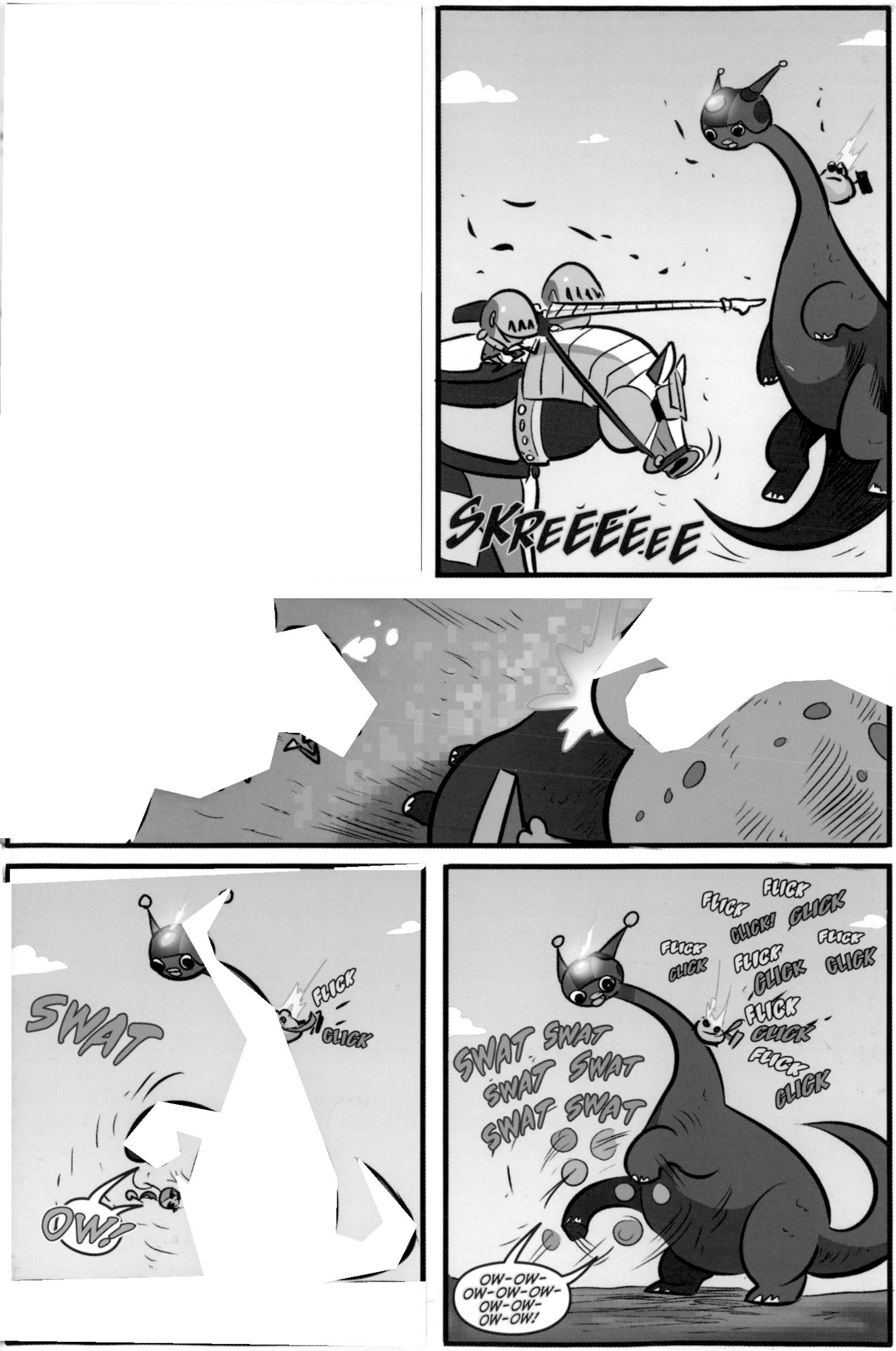
SKREEEEEEE
SWAT
FLICK
CLICK
OW!
FLICK
FLICK
CLICK! CLICK
FLICK
CLICK
FLICK
CLICK
FLICK
CLICK
SWAT SWAT
SWAT SWAT
SWAT SWAT
FLICK
CLICK
FLICK
CLICK
OW-OW-
OW-OW-OW-
OW-OW-
OW-OW!

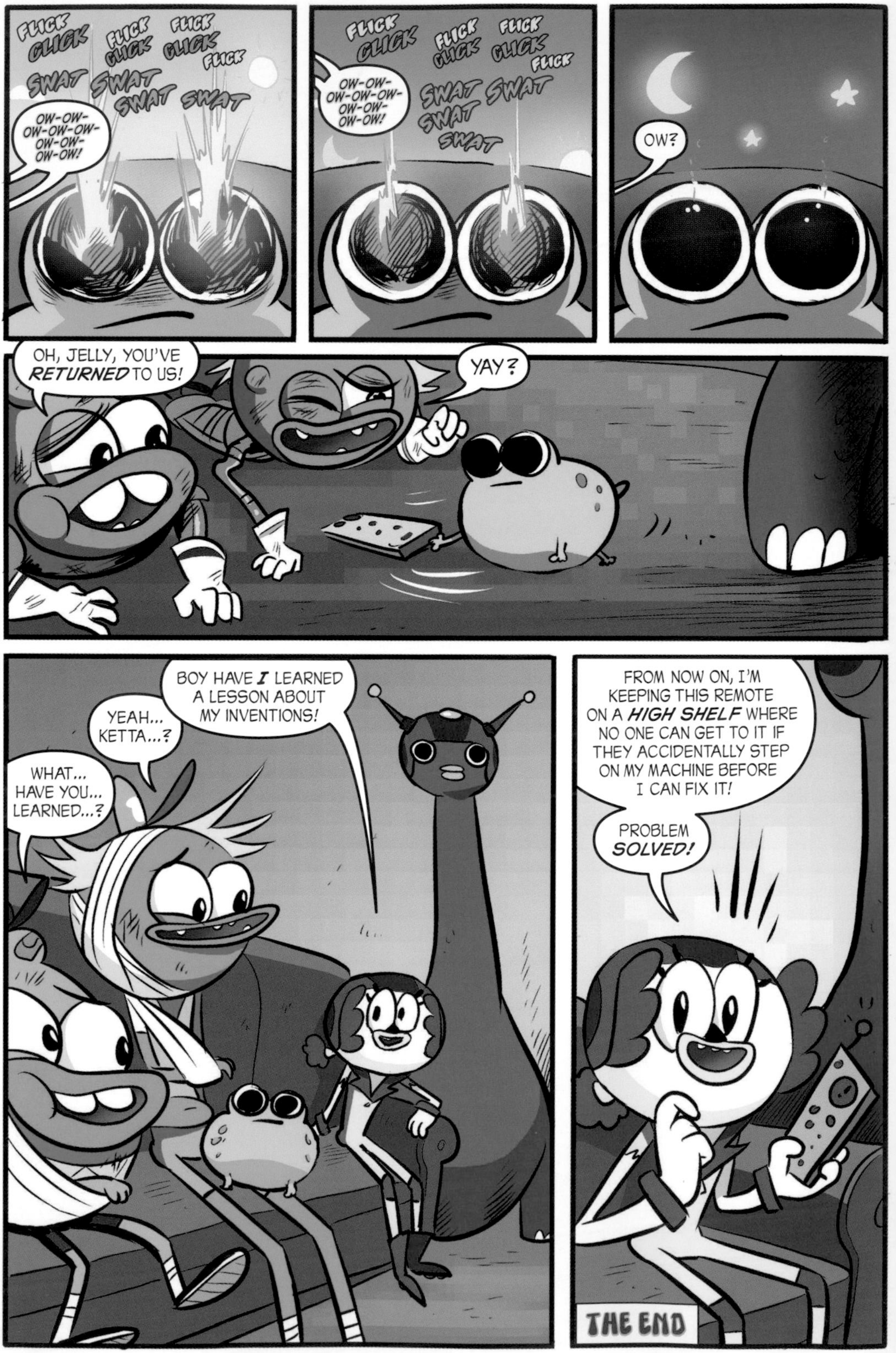
FLICK CLICK FLICK CLICK FLICK CLICK FLICK
SWAT SWAT SWAT SWAT
OW-OW-OW-OW-OW-OW-OW-OW-OW!
FLICK CLICK FLICK CLICK FLICK CLICK FLICK
OW-OW-OW-OW-OW-OW-OW-OW-OW!
SWAT SWAT SWAT SWAT
OW?
OH, JELLY, YOU'VE RETURNED TO US!
YAY?
WHAT... HAVE YOU... LEARNED...?
YEAH... KETTA...?
BOY HAVE I LEARNED A LESSON ABOUT MY INVENTIONS!
FROM NOW ON, I'M KEEPING THIS REMOTE ON A HIGH SHELF WHERE NO ONE CAN GET TO IT IF THEY ACCIDENTALLY STEP ON MY MACHINE BEFORE I CAN FIX IT!
PROBLEM SOLVED!
THE END

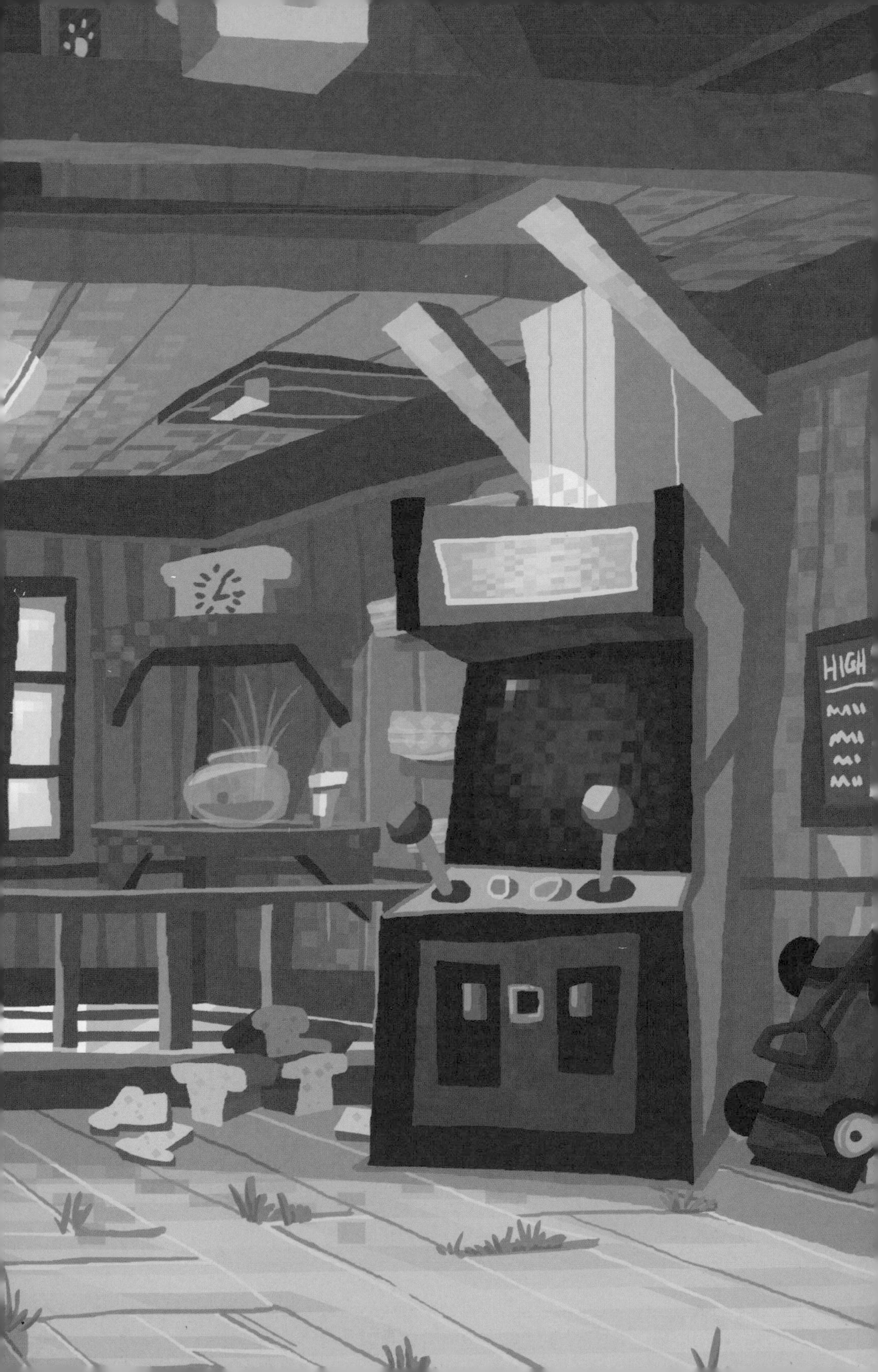
HIGH